FOUR MEN AGAINST TWENTY

Bonner and his three companions were two hundred yards from the campfire when he shouldered the rifle, pointed rather than aimed, and squeezed the trigger. The thunder of exploding black powder rent the night's silence. Three shots in rapid succession followed the report of his rifle as the men who rode at his side emptied their single-shot rifles into the camp. The marauders, fully visible now in the campfire's flames, turned to face the four men who rode down on them.

Four men against twenty, five to one . . . Bonner didn't like the odds. He lifted his revolver and fired, once, twice, and two of the outlaws dropped. If tonight was his night to die, he was going to take as many of the highwaymen with him as he could. . . .

The Stagecoach Series
Ask your bookseller for the books you have missed

STATION 1: DODGE CITY
STATION 2: LAREDO
STATION 3: CHEYENNE
STATION 4: TOMBSTONE
STATION 5: VIRGINIA CITY
STATION 6: SANTA FE
STATION 7: SEATTLE
STATION 8: FORT YUMA
STATION 9: SONORA
STATION 10: ABILENE
STATION 11: DEADWOOD
STATION 12: TUCSON
STATION 13: CARSON CITY
STATION 14: CIMARRON
STATION 15: WICHITA
STATION 16: MOJAVE
STATION 17: DURANGO
STATION 18: CASA GRANDE
STATION 19: LAST CHANCE
STATION 20: LEADVILLE
STATION 21: FARGO
STATION 22: DEVIL'S CANYON
STATION 23: EL PASO
STATION 24: MESA VERDE
STATION 25: SAN ANTONIO
STATION 26: TULSA
STATION 27: PECOS
STATION 28: EL DORADO
STATION 29: PANHANDLE
STATION 30: RAWHIDE
STATION 31: ROYAL COACH
STATION 32: TAOS
STATION 33: DEATH VALLEY
STATION 34: DEADMAN BUTTE
STATION 35: BONANZA CITY
STATION 36: CASPER
STATION 37: SHAWNEE
STATION 38: GRAND TETON
STATION 39: FORT VERDE
STATION 40: SILVERADO
STATION 41: RED BUFFALO
STATION 42: FORT DAVIS

STAGECOACH STATION 42:
FORT DAVIS

Hank Mitchum

Created by the producers of
**Wagons West, The Badge,
Abilene, and Faraday.**

Book Creations Inc., Canaan, NY · Lyle Kenyon Engel, Founder

BANTAM BOOKS
NEW YORK · TORONTO · LONDON · SYDNEY · AUCKLAND

FORT DAVIS

A Bantam Book / published by arrangement with
Book Creations, Inc.

Bantam edition / July 1989

Produced by Book Creations, Inc.
Lyle Kenyon Engel, Founder

ISBN 0-553-28002-3

Published simultaneously in the United States and Canada

PRINTED IN THE UNITED STATES OF AMERICA

KR   0 9 8 7 6 5 4 3 2 1

STAGECOACH STATION 42:

FORT DAVIS

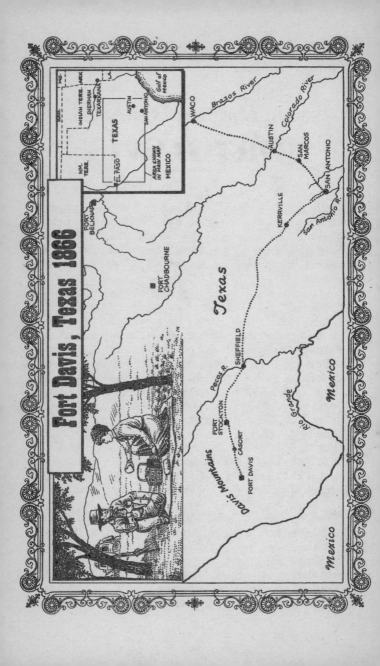

Chapter One

A rifle cracked above the thunder of pounding hooves. *Wade Bonner's pulse tripled its beat until his temples resounded like a runaway bass drum. His breath grew shallow, quickening as he readied himself for the inevitable charge, the advancing horde of Yankees in their blue uniforms.*

Another rifle barked, the report distinct, closer—

"Haw! On with you, you lazy, good-for-nothing—"

Wade's head snapped up, his gray eyes wide. Disoriented, he blinked once, twice, as realization edged away the cottony daze of half sleep. The lush greens of knee-high grass and tall post oaks, their limbs weighted with dense foliage, rushed by him in a blur. His hands, the knuckles strained white, eased their tight grip on the handrails enclosing the roof of the Concord coach on which he rode. This was east Texas, and he was riding on top with the baggage—

For the third time a rifle's blast shattered the day.

No, Wade told himself, drawing a steadying breath. It was not a rifle but the sharp crack of the whip that the stagecoach driver teased above the backs of his six-horse team.

Wade exhaled. He had drifted off, and for a moment he had been preparing to meet a Union cavalry charge back in a meadow in Kentucky—or had it been in Tennessee or Virginia?

He sucked in another breath and slowly released it. It was hard to remember which meadow or which charge. There had been so many battles—more won than lost, at

1

least in those first years. And when the echo of the last shot had died, all had been for naught.

"Haw! Haw!" The driver's right arm shot forward, sending the whip snaking out over the team.

Wade's hands tightened around the rail again. The stagecoach lurched abruptly to the right and then reversed course and rocked to the left in the space of a single heartbeat. The sudden movement threw him sideways, the corner of a woman's traveling trunk biting into his shoulder. He grunted, turned to glance behind the coach, and was surprised to find that none of the luggage had spilled to the ground. But then the baggage—all of it overflow from the coach's boot—was securely strapped in place with heavy leather belts.

He himself was far from secure, but he did not complain about his accommodations. Beggars could not be choosers. The charity of the driver, a barrel-chested man named Bo Putnam, with flaming red hair and a long drooping mustache of the same startling color, was the only thing between Wade's riding and his wearing out boot leather on this same dusty road to Waco. It was also why he sat atop the stage rather than riding inside with the seven paying passengers.

Bo Putnam and his shotgunner, Eulie Wyatt, whose belly equaled the girth of his partner's chest, had put their jobs at risk by picking him up outside Texarkana. The management of the Gaynes Stagecoach Line frowned on employees who gave away seats for which a fee could—and should—be collected. But Bo, the driver of the only coach Wade had seen for two weeks, had been sympathetic to the lost cause of the Confederacy—an unexpected stroke of luck for Wade, one of the few he had received on the long trail home from Appomattox.

Eulie twisted around in his seat. "Waco up ahead, Reb!" he called, jabbing a finger to the south. "See 'er down yonder? Just beyond them trees."

A grin spread across Wade's face. Now the rapid tempo of his heartbeat came not from half-recalled nightmares but from excitement. Beyond the towering cotton-woods, elms, and willows, growing along the banks of the

Brazos River like some massive hedge gone wild, he saw the cluster of houses and buildings, most of them sporting exteriors whitewashed with a mixture of lime, flour, and water.

Bo Putnam glanced over a shoulder to flash a smile, exposing a wide gap where two upper front teeth had once been. A hint of a whistle could be heard in his words when he yelled, "Hang on, boy, I'll have you home quicker'n you can shake a stick!"

To emphasize his promise, he cracked the long whip over the backs of the team three times in rapid succession and urged the horses on with a series of loud curses that Wade was sure would bring blushes to the cheeks of the female passengers.

Home! Bo's word rang clear and true in Wade's mind. How many times had the simple word kept his weary body going when it would have been easier to lie down and give up? Dreaming of this moment had time and again lifted his very soul from the blackest pits of despair. Home—it lay a mere ten miles due west of Waco.

"Hold on to your hats!" Bo shouted back at the passengers. "Bridge comin' up!"

Without slowing the horses, he guided them with an expert touch around a sweeping curve in the road and onto a wooden bridge spanning the Brazos. The coach's thoroughbraces, designed to soften the impact of potholes, ruts, bumps, and rocks on the trail, proved worthless as the stagecoach's iron-rimmed wheels bounced, jostled, and skidded across the structure's washboard surface.

"Heard talk last time through Waco," Eulie shouted at Bo over the near-deafening rattle of wheels on wood. "They're thinkin' about buildin' somethin' called a suspension bridge here. Gonna replace this rattrap 'fore it collapses and kills someone."

A suspension bridge meant nothing to Wade. He was too preoccupied with trying to keep his seat on the violently swaying coach.

Not that Bo seemed to notice. He just sent the whip out over the horses' backs again, and the stage made one final lurch as it left the bridge and returned to the dirt road. Only when he had shot past the scattering of homes that fringed the town did the driver take a two-handed grip on the reins and lean his weight against them. "Easy now! Easy does it!"

Never once touching the stage's brake, Bo used deft hands on the reins and a soothing voice to bring the team to an easy trot as they entered the town's square and then came to a full stop in front of a two-story, red-brick building bearing a white sign with black letters: Gaynes Stagecoach Line, Home Office.

"Waco, folks," Bo called out to his passengers. "Rest stop for everybody. We won't be pullin' out till seven o'clock tomorrow mornin'."

At the same time, Eulie glanced at Wade. "It's been a pleasure havin' you along with us, Reb." He inclined his head toward the office. "But this is where we'd better part company 'fore somebody starts askin' questions that ain't really none of their business."

"Boys, I appreciate the hospitality." Wade shook Bo's and Eulie's hands, grabbed the gunnysack that served as a kit for his single change of clothes, slid his legs over the side of the coach, and dropped to the ground.

He did not pause when his feet hit the street. After the men's act of kindness, the last thing he wanted was to cause trouble for them. He hurried past half a dozen storefronts before slowing to a leisurely pace. A glance over his shoulder assured him that the presence of an unaccounted passenger had gone unnoticed by the management of the Gaynes Stagecoach Line; neither Bo nor Eulie would suffer for their generosity.

A deep feeling of satisfaction suffused Wade's breast as he allowed himself the time to peruse the town. He was not certain what he expected to find, possibly the burnt-out shell of a war-weary, dispirited community. He had seen more ruined towns than he cared to remember during the twelve months it had taken him to walk across half a continent, from Virginia to Texas.

What he did see was a bustling, prosperous settlement. The long years of war had left no mark on Waco. But then Texas had been spared the bloody fighting that had all but destroyed her sister states in the ill-fated Confederacy. Her borders had been threatened by Union armies fewer than half a dozen times.

A squeaking shingle, rocking to and fro in the spring breeze, drew Wade's attention to his right. The sign, Livery Stable—J. L. Beeman Proprietor, hung above the open double doors of a red barn.

Wade dug a hand deep into the pocket of his faded black breeches and came out with two silver dollars—U.S., not Confederate. They were all the money he had. The coins, along with the shirt on his back, his pants, his trail-scarred boots, and the change of clothes in the gunnysack, had come from a widow outside of Richmond, Virginia, in exchange for two weeks of fence building. During the months on the road home, he had vigilantly guarded the coins as if they were a king's ransom. All that time he had never been certain why the coins were so precious to him or why he had refused to spend them— even though they would have bought food to appease his aching empty belly.

Now, looking at the swaying livery-stable sign, he understood. He recognized that an idea had been lurking in the back of his mind for the past year. . . .

It was not fitting for a man to come home with his boots shuffling in the dirt and his tail tucked between his legs like some whipped dog. He should arrive on horse-back, with his head high and back straight!

He smiled as he tossed the sack over a shoulder and started toward the stable. Two dollars would not buy a horse, but he could use it to hire himself a mount for the last ten miles of his journey. It would be a grand home-coming, right enough, his family crowding around the returning war veteran. . . .

But the celebration would be short-lived. Wade felt a cold spike of fear drive into his breast, banishing the comforting warmth of the anticipated reunion. No amount of honorable service to the Confederate cause, he realized, could erase the fact that he was a wanted man. Five years earlier, at the age of nineteen, he had run from the law, accused of a murder he had not committed—and as far as he knew, the arrest warrant was still outstanding.

He had been forced to flee without explanation to his family. What they had been told by others, he could not say. He knew they would welcome him now and remain loyal to him. In Texas, families stuck together. But even so, he could not stay with them for more than a day or two. It was too dangerous, and it could even prove deadly!

He ran a hand over his cheeks and chin. His fingertips tested the thick dark-brown beard that grew halfway down his neck as he once more gazed at the town around him. He silently prayed that his appearance had changed more than Waco's. The beard was his only disguise; it was several shades darker than the strands of hair poking from beneath his sweat-stained hat, which was pulled down low over his face. He had no doubt that the name he used—he had enlisted in the Confederate Army as Wade Bonner and had kept that name—would prove to be a flimsy charade if any of his old acquaintances recognized him. And after surviving a war, he had no desire to surrender or get caught.

Before leaving Virginia, he had weighed the risks of coming home, realizing that they were great. He had decided to take his chances, wanting desperately to see his family, but now that he was here, the fear of being apprehended loomed over him, like a buzzard circling above a dying man. Just one pair of eyes recognizing the man beneath the wild beard would be enough to bring the law down on him.

Two days. He tried to reassure himself that nothing could happen in that time, especially if he confined himself to his parents' farm. Afterward he would move on—head west, maybe cross the border into New Mexico Territory. There a man could make a life for himself; all he needed was a little land—

"Bo, watch out or you'll break your fool neck!"

Wade recognized Eulie Wyatt's voice behind him.

"Bo, you're too old to be climbin'—"

A woman's horrified shriek drowned the rest of the shotgunner's warning.

Wade swung around as a chorus of gasps rose from the passengers gathered about the stage. Bo Putnam tumbled from the top of the coach, where he had been loosening the leather straps that anchored the luggage. The driver's shouted curse ended in a yowl of pain as he fell and slammed into the ground, left shoulder first.

Whether Bo had forgotten to lock the stage's brake or it had worked loose, Wade could not tell. Nor did it matter; the results were the same. Bo's cry of pain and another round of gasps from the passengers were all that was needed to spook the pair of bays at the head of the team. With high-pitched neighing, the bays lunged forward, pulling on the traces, and behind them the team's four remaining horses bolted. Driverless, the runaway Concord stagecoach raced down the narrow streets, swaying dangerously from side to side and spilling loose suitcases from its roof.

Wade acted rather than thought. Tossing the gunnysack from his shoulder, he darted into the street. His original intent was to wave the team down, but one glance at the whites of the horses' wide eyes told him that such an action would only force the team onto the wooden sidewalk and, in all probability, overturn the coach.

Instead, Wade backstepped to the side of the street and waited. When the bays were but ten feet from him, he ran and leapt. There was no time for the team to shy from him as he jumped high with arms outstretched to grasp the harness of one of the lead horses.

Pulling his knees to his chest while maintaining his precarious hold, Wade thrust his feet down. The horse's forward momentum and the rebounding spring of Wade's legs as they hit the ground were enough to send his body sailing upward and onto the animal's back.

With his thighs and calves clamped to the bay's sides, Wade leaned over the horse's neck. His natural inclination was to weave his fingers into the animal's flying mane and hang on for his life. Although that would allow him to keep his seat on the bay's back, it would do nothing to halt the runaway team. The only way to do that was to get at the lead pair's bits, and there was no safe way to accomplish that task.

The pressure of his legs around the horse doubled as he stretched both arms out. The fingers of his right hand found the bit of the bay he rode and slipped around it. But try as he might, his left hand could not reach the bit of the horse harnessed to his left. The best he could manage was to snag a dangling rein.

That was enough. Rising, he pulled back on both rein and bit. The lead bays, their heads drawn inward toward each other, slowed to a trot.

"That's it." Wade's voice was a soothing coo of approval to the animals. "That's it."

The team's pace dropped to a walk, and then the horses stopped. Wade sat motionless, his lips pursed. Sighing, he cautiously released his hold on the bays and slid to the ground. After several reassuring strokes to the necks of both animals, he gathered the reins and carefully climbed into the driver's seat.

Handling a stagecoach was new to Wade, but the coach differed little from the supply and ammunition wagons he had driven during the war. A team of horses was a team of horses, after all, no matter what it was pulling.

Grasping the reins, Wade clucked the team forward, easing the horses to one side of the avenue before swinging them around. The street was too narrow to allow him to make a complete U-turn in one pass, so he stopped the team, tugged the horses' heads in the opposite direction, and backed the stagecoach as far as the street would permit. Then he halted the team again, clucked the animals forward, and completed the turn.

In the street ahead of him Wade saw two men assisting Bo to his feet. The driver's left arm dangled at his side; there was an unnatural twist to his wrist. Wade heard him growl several colorful phrases in reply to the men's suggestion that he see a doctor, but his curses did nothing to deter the two. They firmly led him down the street toward a physician's office.

Eulie stood in front of the stage-line office, taking the bays' heads as Wade drew the team to a halt. Wade pulled back on the brake and then gave it an extra tug to make doubly certain it was locked before stepping down to the street.

Eulie smiled. "That was mighty quick thinkin'."

He broke off as a muffled moan came from inside the coach. Wade arched a puzzled eyebrow and reached out to open the stage's door. As he peered inside, his eyes opened wide with surprise: The stagecoach had not been empty when the team had bolted.

A young woman in a green silk dress with a ruffled, lacy collar lay sprawled belly down on the coach's floor. She raised her head, and a hat matching the color of her dress slid to the side as her chestnut-hued tresses came unbound and tumbled in disarray. Emerald eyes blinked up at Wade, while the woman's mouth gave a funny little twist of disgust.

In spite of her decidedly awkward pose and the tangled strands of hair that fell across her face, she was beautiful, and Wade stood motionless, unable to pull his gaze away. Her eyes were like gems, her nose was small and slightly upturned, while her lips—

"Are you just going to stand there?"

"Huh?" Wade blinked, noticing that those lips moved.

"I said, are you just going to stand there?" the young woman repeated with more than a hint of exasperation in her tone. "Or are you going to help me up?"

"I"—Wade tried to gather his wandering thoughts— "I-I'm going to help you."

"Good!" Her head tilted to one side in question. "When?"

"Right now, I reckon."

Wade was uncertain what she wanted from him, but he did know the quickest way to get her on her feet. He reached into the coach, grasped her under the arms, half lifted and half dragged her from the stage, and set her down on the street.

When the young woman looked up at him again, her emerald eyes narrowed and flashed fire. Her lips quivered, but before she could speak her piece, three other women who had been passengers on the stagecoach rushed forward, hovering around her like a flock of mother hens.

"You *poor* dear!" An overweight woman in a black dress, her gray hair piled high in a loose bun, took the younger woman by her shoulders and edged her toward the sidewalk. "You don't realize how lucky you are to still be alive!"

"It must have been quite an ordeal!" said another woman, primly dressed with a stiff, starched collar that rose all the way to her chin. "I was terrified just watching."

"Come with us." A third woman, as skinny as the first was plump, followed on the heels of the others. "We'll get you to your hotel room, where you can rest and gather your strength."

Wade watched the three hustle their adopted ward onto the boardwalk and into a hotel three doors down from the stagecoach office. He shook his head. The young woman's ride had been unexpected, and she had been jostled around a bit, but he could see no reason for such a commotion over her condition. She had looked more than fine to him when he lifted her from the coach.

A hand tapped Wade's shoulder. He turned, and Eulie leaned to his ear. "Reb, I appreciate all you done, but I'd be grateful now if you just kinda drifted away." Eulie inclined his head toward the office door, where a man stood surveying the street scene. "That's the boss."

Wade needed no further explanation. "Thanks again for the ride." He nodded at Eulie and went to recover his discarded gunnysack. There was a horse to rent and ten miles to cover before he finally reached home. Besides, it was beginning to get a mite too uncomfortable here in town. A crowd was gathering to learn what had caused the runaway, and the more people he ran into the greater the likelihood of his meeting someone he knew. He had no desire to risk that.

"You there!" a man's voice called out behind him.

Wade kept going, bending down to pick up the sack and then continuing toward the stable.

"Young man, stop! I say stop!"

Wade felt a chill of dread running up his spine. As

much as he wanted to ignore the voice, he could not. His heart sank.

Wade's first impulse was to continue on—to flee before the law could slap him in chains. It required all his self-control—as well as the knowledge that a man on foot was no match against mounted lawmen with bloodhounds—to bring him to a standstill He sucked down two lungfuls of air to steel himself for the worst. His heart slammed against his ribs as he turned to face the inevitable.

"Young man, I don't know who you are or where you came from, but I—"

Wade blinked at the man addressing him, and he felt the tension rush out of him. It was not a sheriff who was coming toward him, but the man he had seen standing in the stage line's office.

"—I want to shake your hand for what you just did." The man's words penetrated Wade's confused mind. "You just saved me a whale of a lot of money—maybe even my—"

The man did not finish his sentence. One of the two men whom Wade had seen helping Bo Putnam to the doctor's office came back up the street and started talking to the stage-line official. Wade caught an occasional word now and then, but not enough to make out the gist of the newcomer's message. The man's tone and his emphatic gestures bespoke concern and urgency, and his anxiety was mirrored in the stage-line official's expression. Finally the official thanked the newcomer and turned back to Wade.

"Permit me to start over." The official extended a hand to Wade, and a smile uplifted the corners of his mouth, though the lines of worry creasing his brow remained. "My name's Ramsey Gaynes. I own that coach and team you so ably managed to stop from running all the way to Austin."

Wade accepted the man's hand and shook it. Gaynes's grip was strong and firm. It fit the man, for in spite of his black suit and vest, his gold watch and chain, and his starched white shirt, Gaynes did not seem like a businessman. With a change of clothes and a wide-brimmed hat atop his neatly combed black hair, he would have looked at home in the driver's seat of his own stagecoach. Standing an inch under Wade's five feet eleven inches, Gaynes appeared to have twice the breadth, but Wade could not detect any fat beneath the man's suit. A muscular chest strained his vest, not a flabby belly.

"When I first hailed you," Gaynes continued, "it was just to pass along my thanks for the way you stopped the runaway. But now the situation has changed."

Apprehension tightened Wade's chest. Maybe he was not out of the woods yet.

"It appears I have a little problem." Gaynes pursed his lips and sucked at his teeth. "A *big* problem, actually. Henry here just came from Doc Weaver's. Bo, my driver, seems to have broken his wrist and a collarbone in that spill he took. I'm in a bit of a quandary, because I haven't got another man to take Bo's place."

An expectant gleam was in Gaynes's blue eyes as they stared at Wade. His gaze shifted, moving over Wade from head to toes as if he were studying the lines of a horse he was planning to buy. He stopped short of asking Wade to open his mouth so that he might check his teeth, but he did ask him to hold out his hands.

Wade could barely keep the irritation out of his voice. "Friend, I don't think I know what you're getting at."

Gaynes smiled and shook his head. "I don't know why I bothered to look at your hands; I didn't need to. I'd already seen what they can do. You handled those horses like you'd been born to them."

Wade cocked his head to one side and eyed the man. He still was not certain what was on Gaynes's mind.

"What I'm getting at is a job," Gaynes went on. "I'm not trying to be rude or meddlesome, but you have the look of a man who could use a job, and I just happen to have an opening for a driver, Mr. . . . ?"

"Bonner, Wade Bonner." The lie came easily: Time was a lubricant, and five years had oiled every creak from that falsehood.

"Well, Mr. Bonner, what do you think? The work can

break a man's back. The hours are long and hard, but I pay top dollar for top hands, and—"

Holding up a hand to stop the man, Wade shook his head. "I appreciate the offer, Mr. Gaynes, but I've got other plans."

Disappointment shadowed Gaynes's face. "Are you sure? I could sweeten the pot by advancing you fifty dollars."

Again Wade shook his head. "I'm afraid my mind's set. The offer's tempting, but it's not for me."

Gaynes sucked at his teeth once more and heaved a heavy sigh. "If your mind's made up, then there isn't much I can do to change it, I reckon, though I hate to lose a man with your obvious ability."

Wade said nothing. Gaynes might say he was conceding defeat, but he did not appear to be a man who took no for an answer, at least not until he had tried every ploy he could think of to get what he wanted.

"You did me a service by stopping those horses. If I'd lost that coach, I'd be out of business at this very moment. Since you won't take the job I'm offering, maybe you'll let me buy you a meal as a way of thanking you." Gaynes turned and pointed. "There's a saloon over there on the other side of the square that fixes a steak a man can sink his teeth into, and they serve the coldest beer in town— they keep their kegs in a springhouse."

During his years of soldiering Wade had learned a lesson: A man never refused the opportunity to eat, sleep, or relieve himself, because later on there might not be time. Besides, he had not eaten a real, sit-down meal in three weeks. He nodded his acceptance.

The beer was as cold as Gaynes had promised. The first foaming mug cut the dust from Wade's throat, and the second arrived with two platters heaped with fried potatoes and a beefsteak the likes of which Wade had not seen since before the war. It took all his willpower to keep from tearing into the meal like some half-starved man, which indeed he was.

"I started my stage line after Texas seceded and the

other lines pulled out of the state," Gaynes said around a juicy bite of steak. "Got two coaches making runs from Texarkana to El Paso, stopping at most of the towns in between. Can't make the time they made on the old Butterfield Overland line, not with all the towns my coaches stop at. 'Course, John Butterfield wasn't as concerned with servicing Texans as he was with covering the ground between St. Louis and San Francisco as quickly as possible."

Wade was familiar with the Butterfield Overland route, a long, southerly trail whose curves had earned it the name Oxbow Route. Coaches covered the twenty-eight hundred miles in 577 hours, Butterfield claimed; passengers paid two hundred dollars for the arduous journey.

A large portion of the Butterfield route ran through Texas, crossing the Red River just above Sherman in the north, then running down to Fort Belknap, swinging west through Fort Chadbourne and reaching El Paso before entering New Mexico Territory. Gaynes was right: Butterfield had completely ignored some of the larger towns and cities in the eastern part of the state. Independent branch lines connected those towns with the Butterfield route.

"When the war ended, I had just come up with the money to buy my third coach from another line operating out of Corpus Christi," Gaynes said and then took a swig from his mug. "Since then, things have been going downhill, what with the big lines moving back into Texas now that it's opened up again. It's hard for a man like me to compete with lines backed by big East Coast money."

The ever-diminishing mountain of potatoes and the steak that now covered less than a fourth of his plate held Wade's interest far more than did Gaynes's one-sided conversation. Still, he listened attentively, occasionally nodding his head or uttering a polite "hmmm."

"I'll tell it to you straight, Wade." Gaynes leaned back and stared across the table. "When it gets down to brass tacks, I'm hanging on by my fingernails. If that coach doesn't roll out of here on time tomorrow morning, I may as well fold my hand and cash in my chips, because there won't be a Gaynes Stagecoach Line after that. I can't afford to miss my schedule, not with the big lines snapping at my heels like a pack of wolves. I need a driver to replace Bo, and I'm willing to pay double wages to get him."

"What about the man riding shotgun?" Wade had almost slipped and mentioned Eulie Wyatt by name.

"Eulie's never been worth anything handling a team. In fact, this evening he collects his final wages from me. He and his family are pulling up stakes and heading west. Too many blue uniforms for them in this part of Texas."

"Sounds like you need two men," Wade said. "In a town as big as Waco, you shouldn't have any trouble finding them."

"No problem finding a man who can tote a shotgun, but there's a shortage of men with the skill and experience to handle the reins of a six-horse team. Driving a single mule or an ox hitched to a plow doesn't train a man for that." Gaynes leaned forward, his blue eyes meeting Wade's gaze. "If there was another man in town that could handle the job, I wouldn't be sitting here watching you wolf down that steak like you hadn't eaten in a month of Sundays. I need you, Wade Bonner, and you need me, even if you're too proud to admit it. I'm not offering charity here. What I've got is a job with good pay."

Wade edged the last two slices of potato into a dark puddle of beef gravy pooled at the center of his plate. He let them soak up the rich juices a moment before spearing them with a fork and popping them into his mouth. Then he pushed away from the table, stood up, and extended a hand to the stagecoach line's owner. "Sorry, Mr. Gaynes, but it's like I said before: I have other plans. Thanks for the meal."

As Wade turned and started for the saloon's batwing doors, Gaynes called after him. "I won't give up on you, Wade Bonner, not until tomorrow morning."

Wade glanced back and shrugged. "What you do is your own business, Mr. Gaynes. Now I've got mine to attend to." Tossing the gunnysack over his shoulder, he pushed through the batwings and for the third time that day started toward the livery stable.

* * *

Matthew Thacker lifted the bottle of whiskey from the saloon's table and poured three fingers of the amber liquor into a glass. Resisting the urge to massage the ache in his left arm, the well-dressed, thirty-six-year-old man downed half the drink in one swallow. The alcohol burned like liquid fire all the way to his stomach.

He admonished himself for not sticking with the bottle of bourbon back in the hotel room. Although the label on the bottle before him read One Hundred Percent Genuine Kentucky Bourbon, the taste of its contents said one hundred percent rotgut. He tried to convince himself that a gentlemanly concern such as the quality of the liquor he drank still mattered. In truth, he cared nothing for its quality or taste; what he wanted was the numbness alcohol sent through his veins. The whiskey dulled the pain enough for him to forget about his left arm—or the stump that remained of the arm.

Suddenly the irritating sound of chair legs being shoved over the saloon's hardwood floor drew his attention. An ill-kempt young man in a faded gray shirt and black breeches pushed from a table, threw a sack over his shoulder, and walked through the saloon's swinging doors. The man who remained at the table called after him. That man Thacker knew: Ramsey Gaynes. Thacker had purchased a ticket to Austin with his stagecoach line yesterday, when he had arrived in Waco from Louisiana.

Gaynes was of no concern to him. It was the other man, the one with the full beard hiding half his face, that intrigued him. There was something about the man, something Thacker could not put a finger on.

Shaking his head, he downed the rest of his drink, poured another, and set both the bottle and the glass on the table. He knew what he was doing—trying to hurry the numbness, which never came fast enough to suit him, or lasted as long as he desired. With each day that passed, he seemed to need just a little bit more alcohol to obtain the result he sought. Back in Virginia, where army field surgeons had sawed away the mangled remains of what had once been a hand and most of his left forearm, a shot or two a day had been all that was needed to keep the pain away. Now . . .

He edged the thought aside, trying to avoid the obvious conclusion, as he had so many times during his journey back to Texas. He lifted the glass to his lips and readied his throat for the harsh bite of the liquor.

The rotgut never reached his mouth.

"Damn him!" Ramsey Gaynes shook his head; then he slammed some money down on the table and abruptly rose.

Once more Thacker thought about the man who had left Gaynes's table a few minutes earlier. Whatever he had said to the stage-line owner, it obviously had not set well. And there was something about the young man that could not be shoved aside; it wedged itself in the forefront of Thacker's mind.

Impulsively he tossed down his drink, dug into a coat pocket with his good right hand, and left a dollar on the table. Then he rose and left the saloon, hurrying to catch up with Gaynes.

He found the man just outside, standing on the boardwalk and mumbling under his breath.

"Mr. Gaynes, I couldn't help but notice the fellow at the table with you." Thacker said. "I was wondering if you could tell me his name."

"Huh?" Gaynes turned and blinked as though noticing Thacker for the first time. "Oh, Mr. Thacker! My mind was elsewhere. What did you say?"

"The young man who was at your table. I was wondering what his name was. I have the feeling I've met him before."

"Bonner," Gaynes replied. "He said that his name was Wade Bonner."

"You know anything about this Bonner?"

"Nothing except he can handle a team of horses, and he won't work for me," Gaynes answered before bidding Thacker good day and walking toward the stage line's office.

Bonner. The name still meant nothing to Thacker. Yet he could not shake the feeling that he and Wade

Bonner had met before. During the war? he wondered. There had been so many young men in his command—too many whose names he had last spoken over their graves.

No. He shook his head. He had known no Bonner during the war. He tried to recall the time before he had ridden from Texas fired by the valiant cause of saving a nation. Those years as a Texas Ranger seemed so distant now, as if covered in a smoky haze. If he had known a Wade Bonner then, he could not recall it.

Or maybe it was just the alcohol fogging his mind. It did that when he drank more than was necessary to bring on the numbness. It was doing that now, he admitted to himself. He felt sleepy; that too came from overindulging in medicinal spirits.

Either way, he did not care. He had a hotel room, and there was a bed in it. If he was tired, he could go there and nap. *And why not?* he thought as he started across the square to the hotel. Why not sleep? There was nothing else to do while he waited for the morning stage to take him home to Austin.

Wade Bonner found the owner of the livery stable, J.L. Beeman, with pitchfork and muck basket in hand. After Wade inquired about renting a horse and saddle, Beeman silently appraised him for a moment.

"I don't know whether you got the dollar a day I charge for the rent of horse and tack, and I ain't going to ask," the man finally said. "I ain't one for trying to make money off our boys who've come back from the war."

"Nobody said anything about the war." Wade's right hand slipped into his pocket and closed around the two silver dollars. Beeman had inadvertently set the length of his stay at home by naming the rent on a horse.

"You ain't wearing a gun." The stable's proprietor nodded in the direction of Wade's right hip. "All you boys come back that way."

Wade glanced down at his side. Beeman was right: The Yankees had forced all the Rebels to surrender their sidearms and rifles at Appomattox. They had let Wade keep his hunting knife, but he had traded that for food months ago.

"I don't want to know how much money you got," Beeman said when Wade started to pull his hand from the pocket. " 'Cause I ain't gonna take it. It ain't 'cause I don't trust you or anything like that. It's like I said—I don't want to make any money off you, not after all you tried to do for us. What I *am* going to do"—the man motioned Wade toward a rear stall—"is give you the loan of a bridle and ol' Monroe here. Sitting on his back, bare as it might be, will do a man a lot more proud than walking those last miles home. More'n two-score men have used Monroe in the past eight months."

Inside the stall was a mule. "Old" was not merely a term of endearment Beeman applied to the animal. Monroe was ancient. Gray hairs grew abundantly throughout a coat that once had been sleek and black.

Beeman pulled a bridle from a nail in the stall's door and walked inside to slip it on the mule's head. "Ol' Monroe's gentle, and I keep him shod. All I ask is that you feed and water him, and get him back to me 'fore the week's out. Other than that, he won't cost you a thing."

"I've got two dollars for a horse," Wade insisted.

The stable's owner shook his head. "Don't make me no never mind what you got because I ain't renting you no horse. It's Ol' Monroe or go without."

When he put it that way, Wade could not refuse. A mule was not the mount he had envisioned, but the price was something he could not quarrel with. He thanked the man, took the reins, and climbed atop Monroe's slightly swayed back. "I'll return him inside of two days."

"I ain't worried none, son." Beeman smiled up at Wade. "You get along now. I got my chores to attend to, and odds are you got a ma waiting to see her son again."

Wade tapped his heels to the mule's sides and rode outside, where he turned westward, heading through Waco's streets toward his family's farm.

Chapter Two

Having stretched his six-foot frame on the bed in his hotel room, Matthew Thacker never knew when sleep overtook him. The last sounds he heard were voices in the hallway outside his door, the lazy buzzing of a fly, the . . .

Captain Thacker extended the brass telescope to the full length of its three sections, placed it to his right eye, and scanned the countryside to the south. A smile of approval touched his lips. The Rebels were no more than half a mile away, exactly where his reconnaissance had placed their camp the night before.

Twenty men at most, he estimated while slowly swinging the spyglass from left to right and back again. They made no attempt to conceal their position, but sat in the open by the creek. It was as if they had resigned themselves to their inevitable fate and were waiting calmly for death to claim them.

They *did* know they were going to die; Thacker was positive of that. They had to, for there was nothing else they could believe. They were a token force, one of several units left behind by General Lee to cover the retreat of his main army. He marveled at the devotion these soldiers showed their commander; but then, Lee was that kind of man. Everybody knew it.

How ragtag they look, he thought as he studied the weary-looking Rebs, *not at all like the troops that once faced us*. If their torn and dirty uniforms gave any indication of the course the fighting would take, it would be only a matter of days—weeks at most—before the white flag of surrender was raised.

The condition of enemy uniforms and, indeed, the condition of Rebel troops had no bearing on Thacker's orders. The task assigned to him and the one hundred men under his command was to take the creek and eliminate any enemy resistance they encountered. His sole hope was that the fighting would be quick and clean. There was no glory in one hundred men defeating twenty.

"Lieutenant," he called as he slammed the telescope closed with a palm, "move the men out."

In whispers his command passed among the men who squatted in the tall, sweet grass. They rose en masse like a blue wave thrusting up from an ocean of green. Sunlight glinted from the bayonets mounted on the muzzles of their rifles. Three well-defined ranks surged forward.

The Rebels saw them coming; there was no way to escape that. Yet they held their fire. Thacker's guns remained silent on the prayer that there would be no battle this day, that the war-weary Johnny Rebs intended to throw down their weapons

Two hundred yards from the creek Thacker saw that his prayers were in vain. A thick clump of privet bushes beside the creek came alive. Limbs flew right and left as Rebel soldiers stripped away camouflage from two cannons.

"Charge!" Thacker's order was ripped from the air by the thundering blast of Rebel field artillery.

He did not hear the explosion when a cannonball slammed into the ground ten feet to his left. He did not see the two soldiers whose shattered bodies were hurled into the air. He did feel the searing flame that licked over his left arm, rending—

Matthew Thacker shot up in bed, eyes wide and nostrils flared as his breath came quick and shallow. Beads of sweat covered his face and trickled over the rest of his body. He jerked his head from side to side, reassuring himself that he was in the Waco hotel room and had not been transported through time and space back to that battlefield in Virginia.

He gulped down a steadying breath, closed his eyes, and then released the air from his lungs in a heavy sigh. With his right hand he reached across his stomach to rub the cauterized stub of flesh that extended three inches below the elbow of his left arm. The dream—nightmare—had been so real!

And the pain—the unendurable pain—returned. Massaging the arm did nothing to ease it.

Thacker swung his legs over the bed and reached for the half-empty bottle of bourbon sitting on the nightstand. The surgeons had introduced him to the medicinal benefits of alcohol when they had poured bourbon down his throat before going after the remains of his arm with their knives and saws. Since then he had liberally partaken of that distilled remedy whenever the constant throbbing in his arm flared into unrelenting, white-hot agony.

Yanking the cork from the bottle with his teeth, he spat it aside and lifted the glass mouth to his lips.

"*No!*" The tortured cry that rose from deep within his chest was bitter and angry. "No, dammit, *no!*"

With every ounce of strength in his shaking body, he hurled the bottle across the room, shattering it against the wall.

It had to stop somewhere, and that somewhere would be here, he told himself as he stared at the rivulets of alcohol that ran down the pine wall. For too many months he had wallowed in self-pity, growing dependent on the seductive oblivion the bourbon offered. The drinking could not continue; he was back in Texas now. Austin lay but a hundred miles to the south.

Thacker's eyes closed again to capture the image that filled his mind's eye—Clara, his beloved Clara! She waited for him in Austin, and once he was in his wife's arms again, he would be all right. And he had his son David to consider: The boy deserved more than a common drunk for a father. Yes, when he reached home and his wife and son stood beside him, he would be able to overcome anything.

"Anything!" Determination brimmed in his voice. The

same determination that guided his fingers as they massaged the aching stub that had once been an arm.

When Wade Bonner turned the mule toward his family's farmyard, two blue-spotted hounds—one a bitch with heavy, pendulous teats that bespoke a recent litter of pups—danced around barking and snapping at Old Monroe's heels. A grin spread across Wade's face. Except for the house, which showed a few weathered spots in need of fresh paint, the place had changed little.

That was good. He had witnessed too many changes during the time he had been gone, and this farm was a reassuring link to the past. Seeing this land again and savoring the familiar smells that hung in the air brought a sense of wholeness that had been missing since he had fled Texas and joined the Confederate Army. *Home*. The word felt as good to him now, at twenty-four, as it had when he had been a boy.

A slight tug on the reins brought the mule to a halt before the covered porch that stretched the length of the farmhouse. "Ma! Pa!" he shouted, making no attempt to contain the joy of the moment. "Hap! Sims!" he hailed his brothers.

He waited, expecting the front door to fly open and his family to pour from the house. There was no response. A frown lined his forehead as he shouted a second time, "Ma, Pa, Hap, Sims!"

The door opened—slowly, cautiously. A young man with shotgun in hand and an even younger woman—no more than a girl, although her belly was swollen with child—stepped onto the porch. The two hovered together as if for mutual protection. Their eyes darted about nervously before settling on Wade.

"What you want?" The young man's tone was tight and as shaky as the hands clutching the shotgun.

"Hank and Beth Wright," Wade managed to answer through his confusion.

"Ain't no Hank or Beth Wright here," the pregnant girl said. She sounded as frightened as the man.

Uncertain of what she meant, Wade repeated, "Hank and Beth Wright. This farm belongs to them."

The young man shook his head emphatically. "I never heard of no Hank and Beth Wright. And this here land belongs to the McGarth Agricultural Company. Me and Carrie works this farm for them."

"That's the way of it," the woman confirmed.

"But this farm belonged to the Wrights last time I passed through here." Wade was too confused to think coherently. The McGarth name was more than familiar to him, but his pa would never sell this land to old man McGarth. "They didn't say anything about selling out and—"

The young man did not allow him to finish. Shouldering the shotgun, he leveled the two barrels at Wade's chest while he arched a thumb to cock the pair of hammers. "This here's posted property. 'Less you got permission in writin' to be here from Mr. McGarth hisself, you'd best turn that ol' mule 'round and light outta here."

Wade lifted his arms with deliberate caution. "I'm not looking for trouble. See, I'm not even packing a pistol."

The young man's gaze shot to Wade's waist. His chest expanded with increased courage when he saw the lack of gun belt and holster. He gave the air a little jab with the shotgun. "Well, trouble's what you're gonna git, if'n you don't do like I say. Now turn that mule's head 'round and move on. You ain't got no business bein' here."

The matter of who belonged on this farm and who did not was still an open question in Wade's mind. However, it was not one he wished to discuss with the wrong end of a double-barreled shotgun. He reached up and tilted the brim of his hat to the young woman. "Good day, ma'am."

Never glancing back at the shotgun trained on him, Wade reined Monroe's head around, nudged the mule's sides with his heels, and rode from the farm at an easy trot. Only when he reached the two wagon ruts that served as a road did he turn and gaze back at the farmhouse. The young couple remained on the porch, watching him.

A quarter of a mile eastward along the road, he let

the mule slow its pace to a leisurely walk. Neither Monroe nor Wade's unprotected backside protested at the slower pace, for keeping a seat atop the bare back of a trotting mule was not the most comfortable thing a man could do.

But it was not soreness in his hindquarters that occupied Wade's thoughts; it was the farm. The young couple's living in his parents' home made no sense. Where were his mother and father and his two brothers? They would never leave their land, not unless disaster had struck. Wade had seen no signs of calamity anywhere on the farm. And what about the McGarth Agricultural Company? Had old man McGarth become so prosperous and powerful that he had organized a company to manage his business dealings?

Pondering these questions, he felt lost and adrift. His link to the life that had once been his was broken, shattered in the space of a few minutes. He needed time to think, to decide what to do next.

Pulling Monroe's head to the right, Wade moved off the road and guided the mule over open pasture. Spring rains had carpeted the field in bright bluebonnets and brilliant orange Indian paintbrushes. He paid little heed to the profusion of wildflowers whose beauty would have lifted his spirits moments earlier. His family's unexplained disappearance and the sale of their farm stood at the forefront of his concerns. The more he thought about both, the less he could make of either.

He tapped his heels against the mule's flanks, urging the animal to the crest of a rolling, grass-covered hill. From there he could see, on the opposite side of the rise, a creek that eventually fed into the Brazos River. Directly below him the creek widened into a pool twenty-five feet across and fifty feet long. In his youth Wade had often come here with his brothers to fish for bass, catfish, and perch. As he matured, the fishing hole had provided him with the solitude a young man required to ponder his future, and it was that solitude Wade now sought.

He rode Monroe to the water's edge before halting the mule and sliding from his back. Dropping to one knee, he dipped a cupped hand into the pond, lifted the water to his lips, and drank. It was not the white lightning he had anticipated his father would break out to celebrate his return, but it cut the dust from his throat. His thirst quenched, he stood and let his gaze travel around the small valley that concealed the pool.

"Ain't changed much, has it, Tom?"

Startled, Wade pivoted to his right.

A man, dressed in the rags of what had once been a gray Confederate uniform, leaned against the trunk of a sweet gum tree, the closest one of a copse of ten growing at the northern edge of the pond. A broad grin split his face to expose a mouthful of ivory-white teeth. He shoved away from the tree and shrugged. "I didn't mean to frighten you none, Tom. That *is* you under all them whiskers, ain't it, Tom Wright?"

Wade stared at the man, who pulled a Rebel cap from his head and ran his fingers through a mass of blond hair. His own head wagged from side to side in disbelief. "Roy, Roy Calvert! I don't believe my eyes!"

"It's me, all right, though I wonder myself how come I'm still alive." Roy took Wade's hand in both of his big-knuckled paws and pumped his friend's arm up and down. Although it seemed impossible, Roy's grin stretched even wider. "Tom, you're a sight for sore eyes, boy. I was plumb certain some Yankee'd laid you low by now."

"Wade—the name's Wade Bonner," Wade corrected his old boyhood friend.

"Wade?" Roy hiked a questioning eyebrow an instant before the light of understanding sparked in his blue eyes. "All right, I guess that makes sense, after what happened. Wade Bonner . . . that'll take a mite gettin' used to after all these years."

Wade grinned and slapped his friend on the shoulder. "You'll get used to it. I did."

If someone had to recognize him, he was fortunate it was Roy Calvert. The Calverts had been his family's closest neighbors, and Roy and Wade, born two weeks apart, had grown up as best friends. There was no one outside his own family Wade could trust with his secret more than Roy. And Roy would help him if the going got tight.

"I ain't got much in the way of comfort to offer you," Roy said, tilting his head in the direction of a lean-to he had built out of tree limbs and leaves. "But you're welcome to what there is. Come on, sit a spell and cool your heels."

Wade nodded in acceptance, took the mule's reins, and led him toward the trees.

"I reckon you're just gettin' in," Roy said and then smiled when Wade glanced at him with surprise. "I recognize ol' Monroe there. Mr. Beeman lent him to me when I dragged into town 'bout two weeks back. Made myself a little camp alongside this creek and been livin' off the catfish I can catch ever since."

"Living here?" Wade stopped and stared at his old friend. "Why? Why aren't you staying with your ma and pa?"

Roy glanced away, gazing into the distance. "They passed on, Tom—I mean Wade. Both of them died of the typhoid about two years back. My sister Ann wrote me about it. Not about Ma and Pa dyin'—I didn't learn about that till I saw their graves when I got back—but about the typhoid."

Roy explained that the disease had swept through the countryside after a discharged soldier had brought it home from Louisiana. "It didn't take much time for them to get it under control, but by then it was too late. A lot of townsfolk died, as well as them that were out on the farms. It don't take long for death to steal a life away."

Roy looked back to his friend. "Seems Ann didn't want to stay on with Ma and Pa gone. She up and married ol' Will Boyd and moved to San Antonio. Sold the farm to the McGarth Agricultural Company. That ain't the only land McGarth's company has bought. From what I heard in town, it owns about half the farmland in these parts now, and it's buying up more every day."

"McGarth Agricultural Company," Wade spoke the words like a curse. He started to slip fragmented pieces together in his mind and did not like the picture that formed. "That's the second time today I've heard about the McGarth Agricultural Company. It's just like old man

McGarth to take advantage of others' misfortune. He always wanted to get his hands on Pa's acres."

Roy shook his head. "It ain't old man McGarth behind things now. It's his son. He organized the company after the old man died of the typhoid." Roy paused, looking down. "And there's something more, Wade. The typhoid took Sarah, too."

If Roy had suddenly picked up a bludgeon and struck him in the head, Wade could not have been more stunned. Sarah McGarth! Tears welled in his eyes as a thousand memories that had been a part of him for so long crowded into his head. Sarah had been his first and only love. They had planned to marry, before he fled Texas. While he had long ago laid aside any hope of ever taking her for a wife, his love for Sarah remained undiminished.

"I'm sorry to be the one to tell you, Wade." Roy reached out and squeezed his old friend's shoulder. "I know what you and Sarah meant to each other."

"That was a long time ago, and I was Tom Wright then. Sarah McGarth didn't even know Wade Bonner. She doesn't mean anything to me." He was lying, and Roy's expression revealed that he knew it, although he said nothing.

Wade pursed his lips. The more he heard, the less he knew. Sarah's death, his family's disappearance, the death of Roy's parents—had all of Texas turned topsy-turvy in less than an hour? "What about my family?" he asked. "Have you heard anything about them?"

"After I found Ma's and Pa's graves, I went over to your parents' place, only they weren't there," Roy answered. "A man and a woman I'd never laid eyes on before said they was workin' the farm for the McGarth Agricultural Company. That's all I know."

"They ran me off with a shotgun," Wade said, recounting his meeting with the young couple. Then something Roy had said earlier filtered back into his consciousness. "Did I hear you right? Did you say old man McGarth *wasn't* behind the McGarth Agricultural Company?"

Roy's shoulders slumped as though pressed downward by an invisible weight. "You heard right. The McGarth Agricultural Company is Frank's doin'."

Frank McGarth! The sound of that name awoke a tide of hate and anger that Wade thought had long ago been buried, a bitterness he thought he had shed during the years of war. That those feelings remained within him only doubled his quiet rage. Frank McGarth was the last man in Waco he wanted to see, but if that was what it took to find his family, then that was what he would do. "Roy, I'm going back into town to see Frank."

"He ain't there," Roy said simply.

"Not there?" Wade stared at his friend. "Where is he?"

"Don't rightly know." Roy shrugged. "Some say he's down in the Rio Grande Valley, others say up on the Red River, and still others say somewhere out west."

"Damn!" Wade could not contain his mounting frustration. "Then I reckon I'll pay another visit to that couple back at the farm. I don't think they told me everything they know."

"They've still got that shotgun," Roy warned.

Wade stopped just as he was about to swing onto Monroe's back. Roy had a point. "All right, then I'll wait until it gets dark. I know twenty different ways to get in and out of that old house without being noticed. After those two are asleep, I'll do just that. We'll see what young Mr. Scattergun has to say when he's looking down the barrels of his own shotgun."

"You might get more out of Jace Porter." Roy walked from the trees toward the pond.

"Jace Porter?" Wade asked. Jace was the same age as Roy and himself. In fact, when they were fifteen, Wade had pulled Jace, half drowned, out of this very fishing hole. For years after that, Jace had called Wade his best friend. "What does Jace Porter have to do with the McGarth Agricultural Company?"

Roy turned back. "On second thought, seein' Jace might not be the thing you want to do. Jace has a sheriff's star pinned on his chest now. From what I hear, Frank McGarth played more than a little part in gettin' him that badge. I don't think Jace will be as happy to see you as I am."

"If he can tell me about Ma, Pa, Sims, and Hap, then I have to ride in and talk with him," Wade replied, as though there were no dangers involved. But the risks were very real: Having a conversation with a shotgun might be safer than trying to talk to a lawman.

Doubt shadowed Roy's face, but he said, "I guess you know best. But if I was wearin' your boots, I wouldn't go ridin' back into Waco durin' the day. I'd wait until night. Beard or not, you're still Tom Wright to someone who knows you. 'Sides, I've got a mess of catfish, and I could use some help eatin' 'em."

Roy walked to the water's edge. He bent, and lifted a string of three fish from the pond. "'Bout two pounds each, I'd say—just eatin' size."

Wade knew Roy was right—about the fish and about Waco. It would be better to seek out Jace Porter at night, when there was less chance of someone in town recognizing him. "All right," he conceded. "Do I do the cooking or cleaning?"

"Both." Roy grinned. "I did the catchin'!—"

Chapter Three

"I'd be a lot more comfortable back at the fishin' hole," Roy whispered, glancing over his shoulder. "We could be stretched out and comfortable, just countin' the stars, instead of waitin' in this here alley. Reminds me too much of sentry duty. I keep thinkin' some blue belly is gonna sneak up and slip a bayonet into my back."

Wade chuckled under his breath. "It's your guilty conscience eating at you. We aren't doing anything illegal. We're just standing here like law-abiding citizens. Nothing wrong with that."

"Yep, you're right." Sarcasm dripped from Roy's voice. "That's why we're both slinkin' 'round, keepin' to the shadows like a pair of sneak thieves, and talkin' in whispers so no one will hear us. And we're standin' next to a bank, too. Hell, ain't nobody gonna mistake us for anything but moral, upstandin' citizens of McLennan County."

Wade would have chuckled again, except that he heard footsteps approaching on the wooden boardwalk. He threw out an arm, shoving Roy against the brick wall beside them. "Someone's coming. Get back and keep quiet!"

With their backs pressed flat against the brick, they continued to wait, holding their breath while the footsteps grew closer. Presently an elderly couple, out for an evening stroll, passed by without a glance into the alley, and both men let soft sighs of relief escape their lips.

Roy cursed in a whisper. "I don't know *why* I let you talk me into this. All my life I've been lettin' you talk me into things—even when we were kids. Back then all I ever

31

got for it was a thousand or so switchin's with the nearest willow branch my ma or pa could find."

"You asked to come with me," Wade corrected his friend, not mentioning that nine times out of ten it had been Roy's boyhood antics that led to trouble with their parents. A slipup tonight would result in more than a willow switch applied to their backsides. "There's still time for you to pull out."

"Sure," Roy answered with huffy indignation. "Then who's gonna keep you out of trouble? If memory serves me right, you got a way of gettin' waist deep in trouble here in town."

Wade cast a glance behind them, double-checking that the rear of the alley remained clear. He did not need Roy to spell out his meaning. The last time Wade had spent an evening in Waco, he had been nineteen and had ended up fleeing the state with a Texas Ranger on his tail. He tried to dredge up a mental image of that lawman but could not. It had been so dark, and he had not been concentrating on the Ranger's face in any case. And he had been so scared. . . .

"How long?" Roy's words broke in on Wade's thoughts. "How long you reckon we been hidin' here? Five, six hours?"

"An hour, maybe an hour and a half." Wade eased along the brick wall to the mouth of the alley and peered to the right. The yellow glow of an oil lamp came from the window of the jailhouse across the street. Through it Wade could see into the sheriff's office, where Jace Porter and his deputy were seated by a desk. They were talking, just as they had been doing since Roy and he had entered the alley an hour after sundown.

"Never seen two men with so much to say to each other. Just like some old hens at a sewin' circle." Roy shook his head as he poked it from the alley. "Must be talkin' politics or religion. Ain't nothin' else a man can talk about that requires more'n a sentence or two."

Wade paid Roy little heed as he scanned the narrow street in front of the jailhouse. His excitement over returning home had blinded him earlier that day. There were several changes in Waco he had overlooked.

At the end of the block was Driggers' Feed and Seed, or what had once been Driggers' Feed and Seed. The sign hanging over the store now read McGarth's Feed and Seed. Gone, too, was the name "Brown" from the emporium; "McGarth" had replaced it. A total of five businesses now bore the McGarth name; all had belonged to others before the war.

Calvin McGarth had always been the richest man in McLennan County. Where other men were farmers, he had been a plantation owner, lining his pockets with gold made from cotton. Land was all important to him, and he had snatched up every parcel, large or small, that had come on the market.

Staring at the store signs, Wade realized that Calvin's only son, Frank, pursued more diversified interests, which went far beyond acquiring the rich farmland around Waco. How diversified Wade could only guess; the alley afforded him a view of just a single street.

Wade's gaze shifted back to the jailhouse and the two men inside. He quelled the urge to dart across the street, rush through the door, and demand to know what was going on. What he planned was perilous enough. Neither Roy nor he carried a weapon; it would be tantamount to suicide to go into the sheriff's office armed. And under no circumstances would they enter while Jace's deputy was still there.

"—I'd feel a mite safer, if you'd've picked another place to do your spyin'," Roy continued to mutter. "Folks are apt to get nervous over two ragtags like us hangin' around a bank in the middle of the night."

"This alley's the only spot where we can keep an eye on the jail. I can't help it if it's next to a bank." Wade glanced at the solidly constructed building he leaned against and sighed in disgust.

Prior to the Civil War, banks had been illegal business enterprises under the Texas state constitution. The Texans' lack of trust in banking institutions had been a holdover from the years Texas had been independent. But after the fall of the Confederate States, eastern interests had forced the U.S. government to open Texas to banking.

And what better location for a new bank could there be, Wade thought, than right across the street from the sheriff's office?

Roy nudged Wade's shoulder. "That deputy's gettin' up and stretchin'!"

Wade looked back at the jailhouse window. Roy was right. The deputy stretched, yawned, and took a hat from a peg on the wall. He waved at Jace and in the next moment disappeared from sight, only to reappear when the jail's door opened and he stepped onto the street. Wade and Roy watched as he walked away, whistling to himself. They waited until the man turned a corner and his off-key tune faded into the night before pushing from the alley's shadows and hurrying across the street.

Roy entered the jail office first, with Wade at his heels. Jace Porter rose from his seat behind the room's only desk. "How can I help you—" Surprise washed over his face. "Roy Calvert? Is that really you?" He extended a welcoming hand.

The proffered handshake was never completed. As Wade stepped from behind Roy, Jace stiffened and his eyes narrowed, leaving no doubt that he recognized the bearded man. "I didn't think you'd be foolish enough ever to show your face in this town again, Tom. You know there's still a warrant out."

"I was kind of hoping these whiskers would hide my face." Wade's words were a weak attempt at levity.

When Jace's expression remained unchanged, every muscle in Wade's body tensed. The moment of truth had arrived. Besides the star Jace wore pinned to his vest, a .44-caliber Remington sat holstered on his hip. Wade readied himself to leap across the desk and wrestle Jace to the floor the instant his right hand dropped for the gun.

Jace's eyes rolled downward for a moment and then lifted. He shook his head when he looked at Wade again. "No need to fret none about the pistol. I got no intention of using it. I owe you that much for what you did for me that day at the creek, when we were boys."

Wade released a long sigh and nodded. "I wouldn't have come here, Jace, knowing your position in the community, but I need your help. I—"

Jace raised a hand to interrupt his old friend. "I won't break the law for you, Tom. I'm bending it as it is, more than sits well with me."

"I'm not asking for anything but the answers to a few questions," Wade replied with a shake of his head. "After that you won't see me again."

"Questions?" Jace shifted his weight from one foot to the other and then lowered himself to the chair behind the desk and settled back into it. "What sort of questions?"

Wade paused. Did he detect hesitation in Jace's voice? Was there a touch of distress in the lawman's expression? Wade could not be certain; his own discomfort, awakened by memories of the last time he had been in this town, made it difficult for him to read the man's expression. Finally he forged ahead.

"Jace, to begin with, where are my parents? And my younger brothers? What is the McGarth Agricultural Company, and what is its claim on my parents' farm? And while we're talking about the McGarth name, what's it doing painted on half the buildings in this town? It might help if you could tell me where Frank—"

"Hold on, hold on!" Jace held up both his hands as though defending himself against the barrage of questions. His mouth twisted in a strange little smile, and then he motioned to two chairs standing before the desk. "You always were a mite headstrong, Tom. Sit down and take a load off. I'll answer all your questions, but I got to handle them one at a time."

If Wade had noticed a hint of nervousness in Jace's manner a moment ago, the man's manner now abruptly changed, as he tried to present himself as a "good ol' boy" reliving old times with his best friend. Wade wasn't falling for it. "I'll keep standing, Jace, if you don't mind. This isn't a social call; all I came for is straight answers to my questions."

A frown darkened Jace's face an instant before another smile edged it aside. "All right. Answers is what you'll get." The lawman grew abruptly solemn. "Your parents—I hate to be the one to tell you this—your parents are dead. Two years ago now we had a bout of typhoid sweep through the county. It took your ma and pa, Tom. Both of them are buried side by side out on the farm."

Ever since he first heard that the disease had claimed Roy's parents, Wade had been preparing himself for the worst. It did not help now. A steel band tightened across his chest, and his throat grew dry and tight. He fought back the tears that blurred his eyes. There would be time for mourning later; now his questions had to be answered.

"What about Hap and Sims? They never would have left the farm."

Jace shrugged. "Strange times make men do strange things, and it's been strange times in these parts. A few months after Texas joined the Confederacy, your brothers and Frank McGarth went into business together."

Wade arched a disbelieving eyebrow. "They're partners with Frank McGarth?"

"I don't know if partners is rightly the way it was. The idea was Frank's. He took about five local boys with him and headed south. The Confederate Army needed beef, you see, and for a couple of years Frank and the boys drove herds of longhorns from south Texas to the packing plant over in Jefferson. They made quite a tidy profit for their trouble."

Wade could not fault his brothers for working with McGarth. After all, neither Hap nor Sims knew the real story behind their brother's flight from Waco that night five years ago. There had been no time to explain it to his family. He had had only two choices—run or hang.

"Eventually the ranchers and farmers in south Texas couldn't provide all the cattle Frank needed," Jace continued. "So he moved out west and set up headquarters somewhere around Fort Davis. He could get the cattle he wanted from Mexico, as well as Mexican horses that he sold to the Confederate Army. Again, there was a nice profit to be made."

Wade had nothing against men who made money off

the war. Profiteers had often been the army's only source of vital food and ammunition during the years of fighting, and if Hap and Sims had received a share of that wealth, then all the more power to them. It was Frank McGarth's involvement in the enterprise that sat wrong with Wade.

Jace opened a drawer to the desk, extracted a cigar, and struck a match to light it. Roy glanced at Wade and frowned, as though irritated by the lawman's obvious lack of manners in not offering them a stogie.

Exhaling a thin stream of blue smoke, Jace resumed his story. "The typhoid hit about the time Frank drove the first hundred head of horses up from Mexico. Both his pa and his sister died of the fever, so all of the McGarth land and money became his."

Jace paused to take another puff on the cigar. He then leaned forward, placing both elbows on the desk, and stared at Wade. "A lot of folks hereabouts are grateful to Frank McGarth and what he did with his inheritance. Waco had the look of a dying town until he stepped in and lent a helping hand."

The hand of friendship that Frank McGarth had so generously extended was the formation of the McGarth Agricultural Company. McGarth used his newly inherited wealth and the money from the sale of cattle and horses to buy the land of families struck by the typhoid. McGarth was also willing to purchase failing businesses in town. After the war the purchases of the McGarth Agricultural Company increased, as many families pulled up stakes and headed west to escape the blue-uniformed soldiers who rode into Texas and the carpetbaggers who followed like a pack of wolves.

"There are some who say that Waco has Frank McGarth to thank for its existence today," Jace concluded.

Wade had a few things to say about that, but this was neither the time nor the place. While Jace painted McGarth as some lily-white saint come to save a dying community, Wade knew him as the devil incarnate. "That still doesn't answer my question about the farm. How'd the McGarth Agricultural Company get claim to it?"

Jace shrugged as he shifted the cigar from one side of

his mouth to the other. "Hap and Sims could answer that better than me, but you'll have to ride all the way to Fort Davis to ask them. All I know is that the last time Frank was in town—about six months before Lee surrendered—he was carrying the deed to your parents' farm. Seems Hap and Sims took a shine to the country around the Davis Mountains and decided to stay out west. They sold the place to Frank. The deed had both their signatures and was duly witnessed. I saw it when Frank filed it over at the courthouse."

"And you haven't seen Hap or Sims since then?" Wade asked.

"No, nor Frank either," Jace replied, shrugging. "And that's it. I don't know what else to tell you. You know everything I know now."

Wade could not pin down what it was about Jace's manner, but something told him that the lawman, for all his easy-flowing words, was leaving more unsaid than said. Perhaps what troubled him was the glib way Jace had recounted the events, without stumbling once to pull a half-forgotten fact from memory. The story came out too smoothly, as though it had been rehearsed. Wade also realized that if Jace was in Frank McGarth's pocket, as Roy had mentioned earlier, there would be no way of getting the truth out of the man.

"If that's all there is, then that's all there is." Wade glanced at Roy and tilted his head for him to check the street outside. "I'll be going now, Jace. I won't take up any more of your time."

"Tom," Jace said as Wade started toward the door. He waited until Wade turned back. "I know you need a little time to go out to the farm and say good-bye over your parents' graves and all. But I'd be obliged if you were nowhere near Waco come noon tomorrow. There's still a warrant out for you. I wouldn't like to be the one who has to arrest you, but I will. It's my job now. You understand?"

"Understood." Wade nodded, turned, and walked out into the night.

Roy followed him across the street and into the alley.

"I don't know whether to believe him or not," he said to Wade. "Jace sounded greasier than a snake-oil salesman to me. Whaddya think?"

"I'm not buying his story," Wade answered, hurrying down the alley to where Monroe stood tied.

"Then what's your next move?"

"I'm riding to Fort Davis to see what Hap and Sims have to say." Wade untied the mule and climbed onto its back.

"On that mule?" Roy asked incredulously.

"On a stagecoach." Wade quickly described the offer Ramsey Gaynes had made earlier that day.

Roy pulled off the Rebel cap he wore and scratched at his head. "Mind if I tag along? I don't see no point in stickin' 'round here any longer. With my parents gone, there ain't nothing for me in Waco. I've been thinkin' 'bout headin' down San Antonio way and seein' my sister Ann."

"I'd like the company."

Wade extended a hand and helped Roy behind him onto the mule's back. He nudged the animal's sides to move him down the alley. Before Wade talked with Gaynes in the morning, he had to return Monroe to his owner.

Chapter Four

The heavy tread of footsteps or the vibration of those steps—Wade was not sure which—brought him from a restless sleep filled with battle scenes and disjointed images of his parents, his brothers, Sarah McGarth, and her brother, Frank. The cool morning breeze did nothing to remove the sticky sheen of sweat that covered his body.

Blinking to remove the haze of sleep from his eyes, he stared across a town still cloaked in gray shadows. In the predawn the sky above the tops of Waco's buildings was growing lighter. Sunrise lay at least an hour away. He cursed; it could not be more than five o'clock, six at the latest.

An involuntary moan pushed from his lips when he sat upright on the boardwalk, where he had spent the night, and leaned against the office door of the Gaynes Stagecoach Line. His arms stretched around to his lower back, allowing his fingertips to work at the kinks knotted there. With the clarity of hindsight he saw that Roy and he should have accepted J. L. Beeman's offer to use one of his stalls for a bed rather than camping on Gaynes's doorstep for the night. A pallet of clean straw was far softer than the sidewalk's warped boards.

The sound of approaching footsteps edged aside Wade's silent complaints about the sleeping accommodations. A lone man came down the boardwalk in quick strides. He was wearing a high-crowned hat with a brim like that of a sombrero and tan breeches that were tucked into the tops of round-toed boots. A broad grin spread across the man's face when he called out, "Mornin'."

Wade knew the voice, but it took a second glance before he recognized the man whom he had seen yesterday dressed in a business suit. Reaching out, Wade nudged Roy, who lay beside him, still asleep. "Wake up! Mr. Gaynes is here." While Roy sat and wiped at his eyes, Wade stood up and returned the greeting, "Morning."

Gaynes offered a hand and shook Wade's when he extended it. "I had just about given up on you, Wade Bonner. I was going to take the driver's seat myself if I had to."

"Well, Mr. Gaynes, if the job's still open, you've got yourself a driver—and a man to ride shotgun." Wade introduced Roy as his drowsy friend climbed to his feet.

"Y'all got the jobs." Gaynes did not bat an eye at the prospect of hiring Roy. He dug in his pocket and came out with a key, which he stuck into the office door's lock. "Come on in."

Inside he waved his two new employees to a pair of chairs by a desk while he struck a match and lit an oil lamp. "Can either of you boys read?"

Wade nodded, and Roy said, "Read and cipher."

"Good." Gaynes opened a desk drawer and pulled out a leather map case that he tossed to Wade. "Take a look at that and let me know if there's anything you don't understand. Your route's the wide, black line."

Unknotting the string tied around the leather, Wade spread the map across his knees. Roy leaned close and used a finger to trace the route that ran south through Austin and San Antonio before turning westward to El Paso. Over two hundred miles southeast of that border town lay the Davis Mountains, with Fort Davis nestled among their peaks. Nearly five hundred miles of road and trail separated Waco from the old army post that sat on the northern edge of the Chihuahuan desert.

"Any questions?" Gaynes rubbed a hand over his clean-shaven chin.

Roy and Wade shook their heads, both omitting to mention that neither of them had ever traveled west of San Antonio. Wade also noticed that Gaynes did not question their familiarity with the road they would travel, although he did offer one bit of advice:

"If you have any doubts about the way the road turns, ask at the way stations. I got good help at all of them, and they'll point out the landmarks you'll need. You shouldn't have any trouble."

He went on to explain that the way stations were located every ten miles between Waco and San Antonio. "West of San Antonio you'll go fifteen to twenty miles between team changes, in a few places thirty miles. You won't miss any of the stations; they're all marked by big signs with my name on them."

Wade perused the map again while he did some hasty mental calculations. Including the time required to change horses at each way station and serve meals to passengers, he guessed that he should be able to average four or five miles an hour while on the road between Waco and San Antonio. But as the distance between stations grew greater, the miles the horses could travel in an hour would drop. A man on foot could cover forty miles almost as fast as horses pulling a stagecoach.

Will I always be running teams of horses? Wade wondered. He recalled that John Butterfield had used teams of horses and relatively luxurious Concord coaches only on the good roads near larger towns and cities; on more rugged terrain, passengers and baggage were transferred to lighter-weight, mule-drawn vehicles. Called "celerity wagons" because they were faster than the Concords, these rough-riding conveyances, no more than partially covered with canvas, provided little in the way of passenger comfort; but they had allowed Butterfield's drivers to maintain the grueling twenty-five-day, twenty-eight-hundred-mile schedule between St. Louis and San Francisco.

"Will we be using celerity wagons?"

Gaynes shook his head. "You'll be driving a Concord all the way to El Paso and back with teams of horses both ways. Whether those teams are six-horse or four-horse will depend on the availability of sound stock at each station."

Reaching back into the desk drawer, Gaynes extracted a printed handbill that served double duty as an advertising circular and line schedule. "You'll be expected to maintain the times printed here."

Wade scanned two columns headed "Towns" and "Hours Between." He noticed that the first overnight stop came in San Marcos, a town twenty-two miles south of Austin. Unless he caught catnaps at some of the shorter stops, he would be driving over twenty-four hours before getting a full night's sleep. That he had spent last night on the hard boards of the sidewalk, rather than on soft straw, now seemed triply stupid.

Returning to the desk drawer for a third time, Gaynes passed fifty dollars to both Wade and Roy. "This isn't as much of an advance as it appears. I require my drivers and shotgunners to carry sidearms. Reasoner's General Store carries a good selection. The store doesn't open till seven, but you can go over and bang on the door and wake Reasoner. He'll moan and groan about you getting him out of bed, but he'll be only too happy to take your money."

"Wade said you was payin' double wages for this trip," Roy said. "That go for me, too?"

Gaynes nodded. "But don't mistake double pay for a streak of generosity on my part. You'll both earn every cent. It's not just mail and passengers you'll be carrying west."

The man's abruptly sober tone caught Wade's attention. "What else is there to carry?"

"Gold," Gaynes answered without a trace of a smile on his face. "Army gold."

He paused a few seconds, allowing his words to sink in. Wade now understood why the man offered double wages. Texas was filled with Confederate soldiers returned from the war, and any of them might consider army gold a soothing balm to cleanse away the humiliation of defeat.

"It's payroll gold being shipped to the coast from New Orleans," Gaynes explained. "You'll wait over in San Antonio for a night until it arrives from Linnville. You'll also pick up an army escort that will accompany you and the shipment all the way to Fort Stockton. After you deliver the strongbox to the paymaster at the fort, the gold is strictly the army's problem."

Wade's gaze dipped to the map again. Fort Stockton was more than two hundred and seventy miles west of San Antonio. Although he did not like the prospect of being burdened with the gold and the escort, there was nothing he could do about either. Sitting in the driver's box of Gaynes's stagecoach offered the quickest means of reaching Fort Davis, which lay roughly sixty miles beyond Fort Stockton.

"Any questions?" Gaynes asked for the second time. When neither Wade nor Roy spoke, he slipped a watch from his shirt pocket, thumbed it open, and added, "The stage is scheduled to pull out of Waco at seven o'clock. It's five-thirty now. That'll give you time to pick up the pistols over at Reasoner's and be back here by the time the rig is brought around to the office."

Wade and Roy rose, thanked their new employer, and walked outside into a still-sleeping town.

As Gaynes had predicted, the store's owner berated them for their lack of consideration in waking him before business hours. But the mention of the purchase of two pistols, high-ticket items by any merchant's standards, brought a complete about-face in the storekeeper's attitude. Dressed in a nightshirt and sleeping cap, the man opened his door wide and, lighting their way with a candle, led the unexpected customers to a glass display case that held twenty pistols of varying caliber.

Wade's discriminating eyes quickly passed over the single-shot weapons and three older, five-shot Texas Colt models. At the bottom of the case a long-barreled Army Colt similar to the sidearm he had carried throughout the war drew his attention.

"A mite heavy for my tastes," the proprietor said, noticing Wade's interest, "but a good choice. A gunsmith here in town modified it to take cartridges rather than caps and balls. Care to take a closer look?"

While Roy tested the feel of a .44-caliber Remington six-shooter, Wade hefted the Colt. Whoever had worked on the pistol had improved on its original balance.

"There's an extra cylinder to go with it," Reasoner

said. "I'm asking forty-five dollars for the pistol, cylinder, holster, and box of cartridges."

"I've no need of a holster," Wade countered. "I can tuck her in my belt. I'll give you thirty-five for pistol, extra cylinder, and cartridges."

The store owner stroked his Adam's apple and acquiesced with a tilt of his head. "It's too early in the mornin' to haggle. The pistol's yours for thirty-five."

Leaving Roy to chip away at the merchant's forty-dollar price tag on the Remington, Wade wandered through the store looking at other merchandise. He selected two blue shirts costing fifty cents each and two pairs of pants at a dollar each. To this stack of clothing he added three pairs of wool socks; he had tossed away his last tattered pair three months ago.

Then Wade's eyes were drawn to a display of uncreased hats. A gray-felt hat struck his fancy; he could easily imagine the hat on his head, with a new crease steamed into the crown and the brim rolled just the way he liked it. But the ten-dollar price would come close to exhausting his funds. Instead, he took down a bone-handled hunting knife in a leather scabbard from a wooden peg on the wall. At the counter he passed Reasoner five ten-dollar banknotes and stuffed the seven dollars change in a pocket.

Following Wade's lead, Roy also selected two changes of clothing. He tossed one shirt and a pair of pants on the counter and then stripped down to his longjohns in the middle of the store. "This old gray uniform served me well, but it's seen better days. I'll just wear these." He climbed into his new clothes, leaving the tattered uniform on the floor and telling the shopkeeper to burn it—along with the varmints that it harbored.

They returned to the office just as Gaynes drove the stage up and pulled back the brake. "Give the rig a once-over while I go to the hotel and call for boarding," he said as he climbed to the ground.

Wade raised no protest when Roy offered to handle the luggage boot. His first consideration was the team and harnesses. After running a hand over each of the six horses' legs and ankles and detecting neither heat nor swelling, he examined the leather and chain that bound the animals to the stagecoach's tongue.

Assured that the team was ready for the journey southward, Wade slowly walked around the coach itself. A pleased smile lifted the corners of his mouth as his gaze traced the stagecoach's graceful lines. He could almost hear the reverent tone of his father's voice, long ago, as the man had introduced his son to his first Concord stagecoach, a privately chartered coach that had stopped over in Waco.

The fourteen years that had passed since that day of Wade's tenth summer had not diminished his appreciation of the utilitarian beauty in the stagecoach's design. It had changed little in the four decades since the Abbot-Downing Company of Concord, New Hampshire, had introduced the vehicle. Only carefully seasoned basswood was used for the paneling, while equally seasoned elm, oak, and hickory were selected for the running gear. The wood often outlasted the ironwork on the Concord.

"Here's the passenger list." Ramsey Gaynes's voice broke in on Wade's reflections. He looked up and accepted a yellow sheet of paper containing a list of twelve names, with a tally of each individual's luggage written beside the name.

"Check them off as they board," Gaynes said, passing his new driver a pencil. "Do the same with their baggage."

Gaynes then retreated to the boardwalk, standing there and watching as the passengers began to leave the hotel. Wade took no further notice of him, but instead did as he had been told, placing a checkmark beside the name of each passenger who stepped into the coach and passing the luggage back to Roy, who packed it into the boot.

"Laura Parvin, destination El Paso."

The soft voice, almost a demure whisper, lifted Wade's gaze from the yellow paper. A smile lit his face. The voice belonged to the same young woman with emerald eyes and chestnut hair whom he had rescued yesterday. Wade touched the brim of his hat. "Miss Parvin."

Recognition sparked her gemlike eyes and turned up the corners of her mouth. Her lips parted as if to speak, but she did not have the opportunity.

Roy shouted from the back, "Wade, lug them bags back around here."

Wade flashed the young woman another smile and then bent to pick up the three valises on the ground. When he rose, she had disappeared inside the coach. *Oh, well*, he thought wistfully, *time enough to get to know her later*. El Paso was a long way from Waco.

"Why're you grinnin' like a jackass?" Roy asked when Wade handed him the bags.

"No reason," Wade replied. "No reason at all."

Wade continued to smile. *Laura Parvin*. He knew her name, and that was a start.

Through the hotel's thin yellow pine walls, Matthew Thacker heard the call to board the stage as clearly as if Ramsey Gaynes had been standing in his room, rather than in the lobby twenty-five feet down the hall.

Thacker swung his legs over the side of the bed that had provided no sleep throughout the night, stood up wearily, and crossed the room to a washbasin. Pouring water from a pitcher, he plunged a cupped hand into the cold liquid and splashed it on his face.

The man who stared back at him from the mirror on the wall had changed little in the past years. The face was strong, one that women had always found handsome, even dashing. The neatly trimmed, raven-black hair and the sideburns that framed the face betrayed no trace of gray, even though Thacker had survived thirty-five hard years, first as a Texas Ranger and then as a Union officer, years that would have turned a lesser man's hair snow white.

Little change. The words repeated in his mind, mocking him. The throb in his left arm brought his right hand up to massage at the pain, and bitterness suffused his breast as he lowered his eyes to the partially empty white sleeve that dangled at his side.

There *was* change, although it was not evident in the

face in the mirror. *Captain Matthew Thacker*. He could not repress the caustic bile that rose within him.

Like Sam Houston, the first president of the Republic of Texas, Thacker had believed in the sanctity of a union between the states of a young nation that had survived less than one hundred years before civil war tore it asunder. It had been a noble cause that had called him from his home in Austin; the possibility of dying for that cause, dying in order to preserve the Union, had always been in his mind, as it had been in the minds of all the men in blue.

His fingers worked harder at the stub of flesh hidden by the shirt-sleeve. Death was acceptable; it was being a cripple for the rest of his life that was un—

No! He refused to complete the thought. He still had one good arm. That was enough to pull a pistol from a holster, and he had taught himself to handle a rifle once again. That was reality. The mistake had been believing himself to be half a man; that had led to the bourbon. To indulge such thoughts now would be the first step back down the path he had renounced yesterday.

The image of his wife, Clara, eased into his mind like a gentle spring breeze. The delicate scent of jasmine seemed to waft in the air, the subtle perfume that she had worn the day they parted. He knew that his missing arm would bring no more than a bat of the eyes from Clara, for her love for him was that great. All she would care about was that he had returned to her. If there was one certainty in the world, it was the love that Clara and he shared.

Thacker lifted his right arm, turning it from one side to the other. One arm could slide neatly around Clara's waspishly slender waist. One hand could caress and stroke the summery warmth of her white skin. He was still fully a man; the loss of an arm had not altered that fact. And even greater than the pain left by that cannon's blast was the ache deep within his core. Clara was the only balm to soothe that quiet agony.

The bitterness dissipated as a parade of memories marched through his head. There had been other women during the war, women whose accents came from both northern and southern climes. The opportunities to sample the pleasures they had openly offered had been legion, but he had refused them all. None of the women, no matter how beautiful or alluring, had been Clara. His love for her had been—and remained—that strong.

A smile touched his lips. From their love had come one child, David. The boy, firstborn of what they hoped would be many, had been a toddler when the war had called Thacker away. Now—

Thacker shook his head. He could only guess what David looked like now. So many changes must have occurred during his absence. Clara's letters had often spoken of their son, but words were not the same as being at her side, watching David grow.

Seven. Thacker reflected on his son's present age. The war had stolen a father's right to watch an infant become a boy. But nothing would stand between him and his son's progress toward manhood. He would be there for David as his father had been for him. It was more than a man's duty; it was his privilege.

Slapping another handful of water to his face, Thacker glanced out the window. The first few passengers were walking from the hotel to the waiting stage. At least ten minutes remained before the coach would be ready to pull out.

He looked up at a deep-blue sky sprinkled here and there with fleecy white clouds. There was no way to predict today's weather, in spite of such a beautiful morning. Only a fool tried to outguess Texas weather. By noon the innocent clouds might gather into dark, gray-green thunderheads, or the sun's heat might drive them completely from the sky.

Texas. That one word whispered a thousand promises of renewed life. He could almost sense the power of the land flowing into his body, returning the strength that a Rebel cannon had robbed from him.

And a hundred miles to the south lay Austin. Foremost in importance were Clara and their son. He would spend a week with them, maybe two, making up for lost time. Then he would visit Captain Jess Koop. The Ranger captain had promised him that his old job would be waiting whenever he returned. That was one promise Thacker intended to call in. Ranging—whether tracking a highwayman through the Piney Woods or facing a Comanche raiding party on the plains—was something he understood. It had been his life before the war, one that he had loved, one that gave him a purpose. A man could not ask for more than that.

From the back of a chair near the washbasin Thacker lifted a gun belt and the holstered .44-caliber Colt it held. With his one good hand he had no difficulty strapping the belt around his waist. The weight of the weapon felt good on his hip; the six-shot revolver, with its cartridge loads, was a great improvement over the Walker Colt he had carried before the war. In his coat pocket, he kept a spare cylinder loaded and ready. When a man needed to reload a pistol, time was often of the essence, and it was far easier to slip in a new cylinder than to empty spent shells from a cylinder and stuff six new cartridges into their chambers.

Thacker then took a black suit jacket from the back of the chair, pulling it over his left arm first. The bottom of the jacket neatly covered the pistol and holster, and the gun belt was hidden when he slipped the buttons into their holes. A stagecoach was no place for a man to display the hardware he packed. Women passengers often grew nervous at the sight of pistols.

Finally Thacker lifted a wide-brimmed black hat from the chair's seat, where it rested crown down and brim up. No man in Texas would ever risk bad luck by laying his hat brim down or tossing it on a bed. This was mere superstition, Thacker realized, but there was no need for a man to tempt fate. He put the hat on and cast a last glance in the mirror, adjusting the brim so that it tilted slightly to the right.

Lifting a valise from the floor at the foot of the bed, he gave the room a quick perusal to make certain he left nothing behind; then he walked into the lobby and outside.

Two passengers, both gray-haired women who gave their destinations as Austin, stood ahead of him in the line to board the coach. Five passengers, all men, already rode atop the stagecoach. Thacker silently congratulated himself for his foresight in securing a seat within the coach. The Texas sun could be unmerciful even in the spring.

"Watch your step." The bearded young man Thacker had seen with Ramsey Gaynes in the saloon yesterday helped both the women into the coach. He then turned to Thacker and asked, "Your name, sir?"

Thacker answered and gave his destination while the man—Wade Bonner, he remembered Gaynes telling him—marked a yellow piece of paper with a pencil and then took the valise and handed it to a man at the rear of the stagecoach. Again the sensation that he knew the man lodged itself in Thacker's head as he climbed inside and took the last coach seat.

Where? The question repeated itself over and over in his mind as he watched the young man walk around the stagecoach, giving it one last inspection before climbing up to the driver's seat. That question remained unanswered as the man called out to the team, bringing the horses to life. An abrupt jolt shook the coach as it started forward, and soon it was swaying easily from side to side as it rolled southward out of Waco.

Chapter Five

A change in the stagecoach's swaying rhythm brought Matthew Thacker out of a light sleep. His eyes blinked open to see Laura Parvin smiling at him.

The girl—young woman, Thacker corrected himself—was attractive in a shy, demure way. He estimated her age at twenty, and her accent said she came from Indiana or Ohio. She wore no wedding ring; perhaps, like him, she was a victim of the war. She might have been married and a mother by now. He imagined the town she came from, probably small, drained of eligible young men by the call to war and glory.

"Austin, Captain Thacker," Laura said from across the coach. "We're just entering the town."

"Austin?" Thacker's head jerked around.

Outside, a line of houses rushed by. *Guadalupe*, he thought, giving a name to the tree-lined avenue along which the stagecoach traveled, not thinking of the years that had passed since he had last ridden along the street. Slipping a pocket watch from his coat, he thumbed open the cover. Two o'clock in the afternoon. The driver had brought the stagecoach into the Texas capital right on schedule.

Leaning an elbow on the coach window, Thacker peered out. Ahead, to the southeast, he saw the dome of the state capitol poking above the treetops. The closer that pink granite structure came, the faster his pulse pounded in his temples. He was home at last!

The cool shade cast by the trees gave way to buildings and shops of wood and brick as the coach slowed and rolled into Austin's downtown. From above, he heard the driver talking to the team as he drew the horses to a halt outside the stagecoach office, near the corner of Guadalupe and West Second Street.

The cramped quarters of the coach did not allow for gallantry. When the driver climbed to the ground and opened the stagecoach doors, Thacker could not politely wait for the women passengers to step out ahead of him. Last in, first out was the rule. Once on the street, however, he made a point of turning to offer the women assistance in descending from the stagecoach.

Last in, first out also applied to luggage in the boot. Thacker's valise was pulled out first, and he took it from the driver's hands and then turned to hurry southward down Guadalupe to West Fifth, where he turned right and headed west until he reached South Lamar Boulevard. As he turned onto each new street, its name sprang into his mind with beloved familiarity.

As he turned south again, he briefly considered hailing a cab or perhaps renting a horse for this last leg of his journey, but immediately discarded those ideas. His home lay just on the other side of the Colorado River, and he could walk the mile faster than it would take to find a livery stable and saddle a horse.

Far faster! A broad grin stretched across his face as he crossed the Lamar Street Bridge. Three blocks farther to the south he saw his home—the familiar white wooden structure with its green trim. His steps quickened. *Clara!* his mind shouted what his mouth wanted to cry out. *Clara, David, I'm home! I'm home!*

Two blocks, one, his ever-quickening pace carried him closer and closer while his heart pounded so hard within his chest that he was certain it would escape at any moment. In a matter of seconds, Clara would be in his arms, and—

He stumbled when he reached the white picket fence that surrounded his home. *No!* His eyes clouded with bewilderment as they lifted to the front porch. Something was wrong, terribly wrong. A black wreath hung on the front door.

"Clara!" he called, as he slung his valise over the fence and then fumbled with the gate latch. "Clara! David!"

No answer came.

His heart continued to pound, but his excitement had been replaced by icy dread. He rushed to the porch and tried the door. It was locked. Balling his fist, he hammered against the wood. "Clara!" Still there was no answer.

He dashed from the porch and darted around the house. The back door to the house was locked, and his pounding brought no answer there.

What was wrong? What had happened? Panic gnawed at his breast as he moved around the house from window to window. He could not see inside; the draperies were drawn. Why?

He refused to accept the meaning of the wreath on the door. Nothing could be wrong—not with Clara! Not with the boy! It could not be! For a second time, he hammered at the locked front door. Still nothing. Not even footsteps stirred within. Panic broke over him again like a tidal wave. Eyes wide and nostrils flared, his head jerked one way and then the other. What did he do now? This was his home. He *had* to get inside!

The valise! His gaze focused on the bag he had tossed over the picket fence. Bounding from the porch, he retrieved the bag, and then, like a madman, he charged the nearest window.

Desperation drove him like a bullwhacker's whip cracking above the back of a team of oxen. Holding the valise by the handle, he lashed out at the window. Wood and glass shattered and splintered as the four panes fell beneath the assault. Five times the leather bag rose and slammed into the window, clearing even the smallest shard of glass from the broken frames.

Tossing the valise aside, he climbed into the house. Inside he blinked, his eyes unaccustomed to the darkness. Wrenching back the draperies, he stared around him. He was standing in the parlor, a bright room where Clara and he had spent their evenings entertaining friends and guests, and he had played with David on many an occasion. It had been a cheerful room, but now the divan, chairs, and tables were draped in white cloth like sheets over the dead.

Thacker's head slowly moved from side to side in denial as he moved deeper into the house. Dread sliced into his heart as he saw that the chairs and table in the dining room were covered with shrouds similar to those in the parlor. The bedroom belonging to Clara and him and David's room were the same. What had happened?

Panting with his exertions, he left the house and went to the neighbor's home to the right. When persistent knocking there obtained no answer, he went to the house on the other side of his own. Again there was no response.

Exhausted, frustrated, he returned to his own hallway. He realized that he would find no answers simply by running from room to room or from house to house. Breathing uneasily, he went into the pantry, where he recalled that the whiskey was kept. He needed something to steady himself, to still the anguish that was eating at him. Clara would be home by and by, surely she would, he told himself. He would see her soon; he would just have to wait. To calm his nerves, he would have a drink. Just one . . .

He took the bottle and a glass and went into the parlor. Removing the sheet from one of the armchairs, he sat down, poured a drink, set the bottle on a table beside him, and took his first sip.

"The stable that handles our teams is just down the street." A stationmaster with a face that resembled a crow's slid a pair of square-rimmed spectacles down his nose and peered over them at Wade Bonner. "Take the stagecoach on down to Fourth Street, turn right, and you'll see the sign—Vardeman's Livery Stable."

"Right on Fourth Street, Vardeman's Livery Stable," Wade repeated the directions.

"They'll bring a fresh team 'round in two hours," the man said. He tilted his head toward a restaurant across the street. "Dinner's waitin' for you over at Rosie's, and I got a couple of cots tucked at the back of the office if you've a mind to take a nap."

After thanking the man, Wade climbed back into the driver's box and lifted the reins.

Roy's head poked up on the opposite side of the stagecoach. He rubbed a hand at the back of his neck. "Wade, you got any need of me?"

"I think I can find the stable by myself," Wade replied.

"Good, 'cause that cot ol' Kiner just mentioned sounds mighty good to me," Roy said. "I didn't realize raisin' calluses on my backside could be such hard work, but I'm plumb tuckered out. You don't mind, do you?"

"Go on and get yourself some sleep. I'll probably be taking up that second cot as soon as I get back." Wade waved his friend away, and when Roy climbed clear of the coach, he clucked to the team and popped the reins on their backs.

The six horses moved forward in an easy walk, covering the two blocks to Fourth Street. There Wade swung them westward in a wide turn. A large white-and-black sign identifying the livery stable hung from the front of a barn at the end of the first block. Wade had traveled half the distance to the barn when a man in blue breeches and red shirt stepped from the stable and waved to him.

"I'm Ed Vardeman," the man said as Wade halted outside the stable. "I'm short-handed today. Mind giving me a hand with the team?"

"Not at all." Wade pulled back on the brake before he swung his legs over the side of the driver's box and dropped to the ground.

After Vardeman unhitched the lead pair of horses, Wade did the same with the second pair. Guiding them, he followed the stable owner through the barn to a corral behind the red-painted structure. There both men removed the animals' harnesses, which they tossed over their shoulders and carried back into the barn.

"You'll be running four horses between here and San Marcos," Vardeman said. "I've been havin' a lot of teams comin' up lame here lately. You might be a bit late gettin' into San Marcos, but it won't be by much."

Wade frowned. This news was not what he wanted to hear. Other than an hour's catnap he had enjoyed while the passengers were eating breakfast this morning, he had not slept since Waco. A string of curses formed in his mind but went unspoken, for there was nothing he could do about the situation but accept it. There would be time enough for sleep when he reached San Marcos.

"I can handle the last pair," Vardeman said, tossing the harnesses he carried beside a pail of water in which a bar of amber saddlesoap floated. He indicated Wade was to do the same. "Reckon you'd like to get some hot food in your belly."

"I won't argue with that." The two biscuit-and-sausage sandwiches he had eaten that morning had done little except quiet the rumblings of his stomach for an hour or so.

"You won't have no complaints over at Rosie's," Vardeman said. "She lays out one of the best spreads in town."

Nodding his farewell, Wade left the man to unharness the last two horses and started back down Fourth Street to Guadalupe. He resisted the urge to reach back and rub his hindcheeks. Roy was not the only one feeling the effects of sitting long hours on the driver's board. His journey back to Texas, most of it covered on foot, had ill prepared him for riding in the driver's box. Tenderness twinged through his backside with each step he took.

"Mr. Bonner?" A soft feminine voice questioned. "Mr. Bonner, may I speak with you for a moment?"

Wade glanced up, his head swiveling back and forth. A smile moved over his lips. Laura Parvin stood to his left beside the display window of a saddle shop. He tipped his hat as he stepped toward her. "Miss Parvin, how can I help you?"

Those jewellike green eyes fluttered shyly as though she was uncertain whether her gaze should meet his. "I really don't need assistance." She paused, giving the appearance of someone gathering her thoughts or searching for the right words to say. "I just want to apologize to you, Mr. Bonner."

"Apologize?" Wade made no attempt to hide his surprise. He motioned to the sidewalk, indicating they could walk and talk. "I don't recall your doing anything that requires an apology."

She shook her head as she fell into step alongside him. "No, you're quite wrong. I do owe you an apology for my rude conduct when we first met."

Wade's brow knitted. He recalled no rudeness on the young woman's part. "I'm sorry, but I don't remember anything except your smile."

He felt his cheeks flush. Although her smile was exactly what he remembered, he was not sure he should be saying so. The words had slipped out of his mouth before he knew what he was doing. He had been away from the company of ladies for too long, and he felt awkward. Stammering and stuttering, he finally managed to say, "No, I'm the one who should be apologizing. I didn't mean to be so forward."

"I considered it a compliment, Mr. Bonner."

A pleased light radiated from those emerald eyes, and the very smile that had tripped him up in the first place was on her lips when she glanced at him. Had anyone asked him his name at that instant, Wade was unsure whether he could have remembered it. In truth, he was unaware of anything but that smile.

"It's my apology that brought me here," she continued. Her gaze returned to the street ahead of them as they turned north on Guadalupe, leaving Wade with a hollow feeling in his chest. "I really did act disgracefully back in Waco—"

Wade still did not know what she was talking about.

"—after you risked your life to save me when the stagecoach's team ran away—"

He tried not to smile. He had stopped the runaways without knowing Laura Parvin was inside the coach. For one heartbeat he weighed the possibility of telling her exactly what had occurred. But then he decided he liked the fact that she considered him a hero, no matter how minor; he saw no reason to dispel her illusion.

"—my conduct was reprehensible. Instead of expressing my gratitude for a selfless act, I censured you for not immediately assisting me from the floor of the coach."

"I wouldn't worry about it any, ma'am." Wade grinned. "If I remember rightly, I was a bit rough in the way I hauled you out of there."

"Still, your act deserved more than my rudeness, Mr. Bonner," she insisted as they reached the stagecoach office. "I do hope you'll accept my apology."

If he did no more than that, Wade realized, Laura Parvin would walk away, and they might not share more than a dozen words for the rest of trip. He was not willing to risk that. "I accept your apology—on one condition."

"Condition?" Her head snapped up and a thin eyebrow arched above her right eye. For the first time, Wade realized there was more than shyness to Laura Parvin's manner. The challenge in her expression said that she would be quite a match if he ever locked horns with her.

"Lunch," Wade said. "Apology accepted, if you'll let me buy you lunch."

The defiance vanished from her eyes, and she smiled demurely again. "Your condition is accepted, Mr. Bonner."

"There's one more condition," he added as they walked across the street to the restaurant. "The name's Wade, not Mr. Bonner, Miss Parvin."

Though propriety required a formal introduction between a man and woman before they called each other by their given names, she seemed unconcerned. "Wade," she said firmly, as if testing the feel of his name. "If you wish to be called Wade, then I shall respect that wish."

He hoped that she would reciprocate by allowing him to call her Laura. She did not, leaving him with the awkwardness of "Miss Parvin." And for some reason that he did not quite understand, referring to her as Miss Parvin was as irritating as a burr under a saddle blanket.

Inside the restaurant a rotund woman with black hair wrapped in a tight bun introduced herself as Rosie and then led the couple to a round table covered with a red and white gingham tablecloth. "Menu for today is chicken 'n dumplin's, mustard greens, and cornbread."

Since the woman offered no other selection, both Wade and Laura ordered the day's fare. Rosie disappeared through a door at the rear of the restaurant, and before either Wade or Laura could speak, the woman reappeared carrying two plates piled high with food, which she placed before them.

"It smells good," Laura offered while she arranged a napkin on her lap and lifted a fork.

Wade, who was raising his own napkin to tuck it into his collar, immediately dropped his hands and spread the napkin across his lap. He silently reprimanded himself for forgetting the table manners his mother had taught him. He noted which fork the young woman selected from beside her plate and followed suit.

She took a tentative taste of mustard greens.

"These taste similar to spinach," she said with a surprised smile.

"Better than spinach," Wade replied. "I never had much of a taste for spinach—too gritty. I always like collard or mustard greens the best, especially when they're made with bacon grease like these."

"Collard?" She looked up at him. "I don't believe that I've ever heard of collard greens."

"You haven't?" Disbelief filled his voice. "Where are you from, anyway?"

That smile returned to her face. "I was born and raised in Ohio—in a town near Cincinnati."

The shyness he had sensed earlier disappeared as she spoke of her home, of a mother who had died when she was ten years old, and of an older brother who had been killed during the battle of Bull Run, as the Yankees called it. "My father and I are all that remain of our family. That's why I am en route to El Paso. My father is a colonel in the army, and he's stationed at Fort Bliss."

Although Wade could not escape the pleasing sound of her voice, it was Laura Parvin's face that made him all but forget the meal on his plate. It was the most animated face he had ever seen. When she smiled, it was like bright sunshine. A frown evoked images of thunderstorms. And when she mentioned her doubts about the long journey across Texas, Wade could almost share her fears.

"When it comes to the world, Mr.—Wade, I am an

innocent," she said. "Except for attending finishing school in New York State, I have never been more than fifty miles from my home. The newspaper accounts of the frontier are filled with stories of bloody Indian massacres, and robberies and shootings. Surely you have read of the deeds of Jesse and Frank James."

"This is Texas, not Kansas or Missouri. The James brothers don't ride this far south. Besides, banks are new to the state, and they haven't got that much money yet." He went on to explain that although Texas held many real dangers, it was nature rather than man that posed the greatest threat to life.

"What of the Indians?" she asked. "I've read about the Comanches, Kiowas, and Apaches."

Indians were a *very* real danger; there was no way for Wade to sidestep the possibility of attack. "Comanches and Kiowas ride together. But most of their bands have been driven out of the part of Texas we'll be traveling through. They keep their camps in the plains to the northwest, for the most part."

He did not lie, only failed to mention that Comanche raiding parties struck wherever and whenever they wanted, often riding a hundred miles in a night. However, when Comanche warriors rode out of the plains, they usually struck the more populous communities, where more plunder was available. There were few ranches or farms along the trail the stagecoach would travel, and if they encountered any Comanches, it would be by accident rather than design on the part of the braves.

"And Apaches?" she pressed.

"Lipan Apaches used to be a problem," he explained. "But the army drove most of them from the state before the war. A man has to travel into New Mexico Territory to find Apaches."

His words brought an expression of relief to her face. That was just as well; the unyielding sun and rugged terrain of Texas would provide enough worries before the stagecoach reached El Paso—or his own destination of Fort Davis.

"What about you?" Laura paused with a dumpling speared on her fork. "Have you always driven a stagecoach?"

Wade grinned and shook his head. "This is my first time in a driver's box. I spent the last few years in a gray uniform." He paused, looking down. "I'm sorry about your brother, ma'am. I wasn't at Bull Run, if that helps."

She nodded, accepting his sympathy, but went on at once to other questions about his past. Evidently for her the war was over and best forgotten. For his part he avoided answers by speaking of the future and of his plans to start a spread in New Mexico. She seemed satisfied and pressed no further.

Nor did she have time: Kiner, Austin's stationmaster, entered the restaurant to announce the stagecoach was ready to continue southward.

After paying for their meals, Wade helped Laura from the table and escorted her outside to the waiting stage. "Miss Parvin, I appreciated the company over lunch," he said as she climbed into the coach.

"I should be thanking you, since I was your guest," she answered. "And Wade—my name is Laura."

A silly ear-to-ear grin spread across Wade's face when he turned to take a new passenger list from Kiner's hands. Of the men and women boarding, only five were listed as continuing beyond San Antonio. Wade gave special heed to their faces as they climbed into the coach, since all would be his wards for days to come.

Laura, of course, was first, traveling all the way to Fort Bliss in El Paso to join her father. Next came Howard Dalrymple, a nattily dressed windmill salesman who stood five foot six, including the black derby he wore on his head. The jovial man's destination was also El Paso.

Turning down a seat inside the coach in preference for one on top was Deke Harris. Harris's appearance differed little from Wade's before Ramsey Gaynes had provided him the money for new clothes. Rough and unkempt, he might have been one of the thousands of men who were finding their way back home after the war.

Except for the pistol strapped to his waist, Wade thought, as the man climbed to the stagecoach roof. Confederate soldiers had been stripped of their weapons before being allowed to return to their homes. No Union soldier was as poor as Harris appeared. Wade mentally pigeonholed him as a drifter headed west in search of employment on one of the ranches near the Mexican border, since his destination was Fort Davis.

"I want to ride up on top, too." A young boy violently protested by trying to jerk away from a matronly woman who attempted to help him into the coach.

"David!" Exasperation filled the woman's voice. Her arm snaked out to snatch the back of the boy's collar before he could scamper to the top of the stagecoach like a monkey. "No, you don't, young man! You're riding inside with me!"

Wade glanced at his passenger list; all but a woman named Vera Brown had boarded, so this had to be she. The boy was simply listed as "and nephew."

"Mrs. Brown, let me help," Wade offered.

When the woman—whom Wade placed in her early forties—nodded her thanks, he leaned and whispered in the boy's ear, "Do like your aunt says, and once we start west, I'll talk with her. I think I can convince her to let you ride up in the driver's box with me and Roy there."

The boy glanced at Roy, eyed Wade, and then stared up at the driver's seat. When he turned back to Wade, his brown eyes were wide with anticipation. "Promise?"

"Promise," Wade assured him.

"Spit on it to seal the promise?"

Wade spat into his right palm, as did the boy. A wide grin beamed up at Wade when they shook hands. The boy then climbed aboard the stage without another complaint.

"I don't know what you said to him," Mrs. Brown said, "but I thank you. I hope it'll work all the way to Fort Stockton."

"With a little help from you, it just might," Wade answered.

The woman brushed from her forehead a stray strand of black hair, interwined with traces of silver. She gave Wade a quizzical look but did not question his meaning as she boarded the coach.

"We're wasting sunlight," Wade called to Roy as he closed the stagecoach door. "Let's move this rig out!"

From the depths of his consciousness, Matthew Thacker heard a loud knocking and then a metallic click, the sound of a key being inserted into a lock. Groggily he raised his head and looked around. The bottle of whiskey was on the table beside him. He had not drunk it all, but he had had enough to make him sleep. It was dark now; how much time had gone by?

He got up from his chair, his head spinning slightly, and went into the hallway. Hope rose within him. "Clara?"

The front door swung inward. Not Clara, but a man's figure, dimly visible, stood in the open door.

"Matthew? Matthew, is that you?"

The male voice was vaguely familiar to Thacker, but he could not give it a name. All he managed was a mumbled "Yes."

"Matthew"—the man stepped into the house—"it's me, Charlie Powell. Why are you here in the dark? When did you get in?"

"Charlie?" The name and voice fit, but Thacker's mind refused to focus on either. "Clara? Where's Clara?"

"You'd better come home with me." The man walked down the hall to take Thacker's arm. "Bess has some hot coffee on the stove, and there'll be some supper, too. It'll be good for you."

"Clara?" Thacker mumbled again, but said nothing when the thin man led him from the house to a waiting carriage. Charlie and Bess, old friends from the church that Clara and Matthew had attended, lived a dozen blocks away.

Thacker paid no attention to his surroundings as the carriage proceeded to the Powell home, where he was helped down and then escorted along the walk to the door.

"This isn't any way for a man to come home," Powell said, as he guided his friend into his cluttered parlor. "It isn't right at all." He helped Thacker into an overstuffed chair and then called for his wife to bring a cup of coffee.

Thacker, his mind dazed and barely able to comprehend what was happening around him, sat motionless and stared at the throw rug beneath his feet.

Bess Powell, a woman as thin and gray haired as her husband, entered with a mug, which she placed in Thacker's hand. "Here you go, Matthew. You just drink as much of this as you can. It's hot, so you be careful now."

Uncertain of what else to do, Thacker drank, heedless of the coffee's scalding heat. "Clara? Where is Clara?"

Charlie Powell slipped a protective arm around his wife's waist and drew her close while he shook his head. "It isn't good, Matthew. It isn't good."

"Clara has passed on, Matthew," his wife said. "It was a week ago."

"A female ailment," Charlie added. "Doc Thompson had been looking after her for a month, but there wasn't anything he could do. She just got weaker and weaker until one night she went to sleep and never woke."

"Clara—dead?" Thacker's eyes lifted to the couple. His worst fear, the horror his brain had fought to reject, could no longer be denied. "Dead?"

"She was buried four days ago, Matthew," Charlie answered with a nod of his head.

"It was a beautiful funeral," Bess said quickly. "She looked so natural, just like she was sleeping. All the ladies from the church helped out."

"Your sister's taken the boy to Fort Stockton for the time being," Charlie put in. "They left on the stage today—"

Thacker's trembling fingers could no longer hold the mug. It slipped suddenly, spilling coffee over the throw rug. He did not notice. His face was buried in his one good hand. And he cried for Clara, cried for David—and for himself.

Chapter Six

The fiery golds and oranges of sunset were fading as Wade reined his team into San Antonio. A shiver worked along his spine as he drew the horses to a halt before the stagecoach office. In the distance, barely visible in the gathering darkness, stood the Alamo. So many men had given so dearly in that ancient mission during Texas's fight for independence from Mexico; no Texan could look upon those ruins without remembering their sacrifice.

"You! Are you asleep up there?"

Wade's head turned to the office, where a man stood calling to him from the open doorway. "It's getting dark. Time your passengers were settled for the night and your team was put away."

"Right." Wade climbed from the driver's box and opened the coach while Roy began unloading baggage from the rear boot.

Within ten minutes, passengers who would be continuing westward were heading toward a boardinghouse that sat near the banks of the San Antonio River, while others were going their own way. Both Wade and Roy once more took their places on the driver's seat and drove to a livery stable five blocks from the office.

"I'm gonna try to find my sister Ann's home this evenin'." Roy pulled a folded piece of worn paper from his shirt pocket. It was the last letter he had received from Ann before the war ended, and he unfolded it and read her address aloud. "Care to go with me?"

"If you'll give me a chance to bathe and shave first." Wade pulled the team up in front of the stable, turning horses and stagecoach over to three men who ran out from the structure.

Roy lowered his head and sniffed at himself. His nose wrinkled when he looked at Wade. "Reckon you got a point there. This shirt is startin' to smell a mite ripe."

"Could be it's the man under that shirt that's beginning to smell that way," Wade suggested as they stepped from the stagecoach. "You haven't had a bath since Waco."

Indignation stiffened Roy's spine. "But it ain't Saturday night yet!"

Wade hid his smile behind a hand as he rubbed at the beard covering his cheeks. "Saturday night or not, I think Ann would appreciate visitors with less of an aroma to them."

Roy cocked his head to one side, as if he were considering his friend's words. Finally he nodded in acquiescence. "All right, maybe you got a point there, slim as it might be. It's been a while since I last saw Ann, and I guess it won't hurt none to bathe, maybe even shave. After all, this will be a family reunion of sorts."

This time Wade turned his head to conceal his amusement; Roy seemed to feel he had to justify taking a bath—as if soap and water were sinful indulgences that good, God-fearing men used sparingly.

Still smiling to himself, Wade approached one of the men handling the team and obtained directions to a public bathhouse. Ten minutes and two dimes later, both Roy and he sat soaking in a steaming tub of water while they lathered their bodies.

Although San Antonio's barbershops were closed, an extra nickel bought each man the use of a pair of scissors, a razor, strap, shaving brush, and mug of soap. After drying off following his bath, Wade stood examining his face for several minutes in a mirror on the bathhouse wall. In spite of the wildness of his beard, he had grown accustomed to the whiskers over the months. On the other hand, the reason for those whiskers had passed. He no longer needed a disguise to hide his face from old aquaintances in Waco.

Picking up the scissors, he trimmed his beard as

closely as he could, leaving a stubble that would need the razor's attention. Then he took the shaving mug and added a few drops of water to the cake of soap within, whipping up a lather with the brush and spreading it thickly over his cheeks, chin, and neck. He opened the razor and for the next ten minutes painfully scraped away the remains of his facial hair.

"I don't know." Roy critically eyed his friend from where he lay soaking in the tub. "I'll be darned if I didn't like you better with that ugly face all covered up."

Snatching a towel from a peg on the wall, Wade threw it at Roy. "You might consider doing something about your own face. A shave just might convince Ann that she doesn't have a wild man for a brother."

Sighing wearily, Roy stood up from the soapy bathwater, dried himself, and took up his razor and mug. "The trials a good man must endure for his family."

While Roy applied soap and the razor to his face, Wade dressed and then used the soap and bath water to wash his and Roy's dirty clothing. He rinsed the clothes with a pail of fresh water, and by the time Roy had dressed and was comparing the smoothness of his cheeks to "a baby's backside," Wade had wrung out the laundry and left it to dry inside the stagecoach office. Then the two friends began their trek through San Antonio's streets in search of the address on Roy's letter.

A mile west along the San Antonio River, the two found a white, flat-board house with a cedar roof and yellow trimming that bore the same number as the letter's return address. Although no fence surrounded the home, a neatly manicured lawn of St. Augustine grass was bordered by day lilies whose orange flowers had closed for the night. The same plants lined each side of a flagstone walk that led from the street to the front porch. Flowerbeds running in front of that porch were a profusion of reds and pinks. The soft yellow glow of burning oil lamps came from the house's curtained windows.

Roy stopped at the head of the flagstone walk, edged back his Rebel cap, and scratched at his head as he studied the house. "The addresses match up, but I don't know if this is the place."

"It has to be," Wade said, double-checking the letter and the house.

"But Ann married Will Boyd." Roy continued to stare at the house. "Ain't no Boyd I ever known lived this high on the hog. Take a gander at that house, Wade. That don't look like the Boyd farm back home. Does it to you? Hell, the Boyds used burlap bags for curtains—these here are all lace and silky."

Wade smiled, amused by his friend's lack of faith in his new brother-in-law. "Times change, Roy."

"Yeah, but Boyds don't."

"Well, there's one way to make sure," Wade suggested. "Walk up and knock on the door."

Tilting his head in agreement, Roy, with Wade at his side, walked onto the porch and rapped on the door.

"Be right there!" a woman called from inside.

A wide grin spread across Roy's face. "It's Ann! I'd know that voice anywhere! Lordy, I never thought anything would sound so go—"

The door opened. Brother and sister stood frozen for a moment, mouths agape, eyes locked on each other as they stared in disbelief. Ann came to life first, throwing her arms around Roy's neck and planting a loud kiss on his cheek. Then she was hugging, laughing, and crying all at once, and calling to her husband to come welcome her brother. Roy returned the hugs, kisses, and tears in full measure, and even Wade received a barrage of kisses and squeezes and then nearly had his arm pumped out of its socket when Will Boyd finally appeared on the porch.

"If I'd known you two were coming, I'd've picked up a jug, and we'd do some *real* celebrating," Will said as he ushered his two guests into the house.

"Oh, Will, these boys don't need moonshine. They're hurting for real food." Ann poked Roy's side with a finger. "Look at this: You can see his ribs sticking out through that shirt!"

Neither Roy nor Wade protested when Ann hustled them along a hall and into the kitchen, where she seated them at a table. Within a matter of minutes she had set before her unexpected guests a platter of *cabrito*, as well as bowls of pinto beans and chiles, a dish of creamed corn, and a plate of hot cornbread. While brother and sister relived old times, Wade's attention centered on the *cabrito*. He had forgotten how sweet and tender the barbecued meat of a kid could taste.

"—I was lucky finding the job I did." Wade half listened to Will Boyd explaining his job as a clerk in one of San Antonio's new banks. "It's a real step up. When I got back from Fort Davis, I didn't have two pennies to rub together."

Wade's head snapped up. "Fort Davis? You were in Fort Davis?"

Will nodded. "I rode there with Frank McGarth and several of the men from Waco. We were after Mexican horses and cattle to sell to the army. Frank promised we'd all get rich."

Ann snorted with disgust. "Nobody's going to get rich working with Frank McGarth except Frank McGarth. That man's worse than his father. He wants to own all of Texas."

Will's head bobbed in agreement. "Or at least all of Waco, by hook or by crook. How he gets it doesn't matter to him, just as long as he gets it."

"McGarth Agricultural Company?" Wade asked.

"That's just a fancy way of saying Frank McGarth," Will replied.

The feast Ann had placed before him was forgotten as Wade leaned forward, his elbows on the table. "Jace Porter led us to believe that Frank had single-handedly saved Waco."

"Jace is so deep in Frank's hip pocket I wouldn't believe him if he said it was daylight unless I could see the sun shining." Bitterness lay thick on Ann's voice as she spoke. "When Frank McGarth says jump, Jace asks which way."

Wade's eyes narrowed as he remembered thinking that Jace had been trying to hide something from him. "What about the others in Waco? Jace gave us the impression that most of the town supports Frank."

"Only the ones trying to get rich by riding Frank's coattails," Will replied. "The thing they don't realize is that Frank's using 'em. Soon as they serve his purpose, he'll buy 'em out or run 'em off the way he's been doing with the farmers."

Frank McGarth was a strange one, Ann went on to say. Reared as a southern gentleman, he had fancy manners, fine clothes, and a certain fastidiousness, yet his acquisitive streak was so broad that it made him look more like a Yankee carpetbagger than a southern aristocrat. And he had a cruel side, too. People said he had always loved hunting and killing in any form—deer, bear, runaway slaves—he had shot them all with equal pleasure. Though he prided himself on doing it with a certain flair, the fact remained that he lost no opportunity to ride at the head of his own outlaw gang. But property remained his chief lust.

"What about our farm?" The question came from Roy, whose expression said he was less than happy over what he heard. "Did Frank run you off?"

Ann's eyes avoided her brother's gaze. "I wanted to stay, but it was easier to sell and move on after Ma and Pa died. The money I got wasn't much, but it was enough for Will and me to start over here in San Antonio."

She explained that she had seen how Frank dealt with those who defied him. "The Shaws and the Egans both lost their farms when Frank hired some big lawyers out of Austin. Seems old man McGarth had loaned Tim Shaw and Howie Egan some money years ago. Frank called in those debts when they wouldn't sell out to him. When they left Waco, they didn't have anything but the clothes on their backs."

"Then there's your pa," Will added. "He tried to hold out after the typhoid took your mother. Didn't get him anywhere but dead."

Wade blinked, not certain he had understood the man. "Jace said Pa died of typhoid just like Ma."

"It wasn't any more typhoid than it was lead poisoning," Ann replied with a determined shake of her head, "unless you want to call three bullets in the back lead poisoning. Your pa was murdered. It's that plain and

simple. They found his body in a drainage ditch outside
Waco three days after your ma died."

"Shot down. . . ." Wade mumbled as his mind reeled
under the impact of Ann's words. "Was it Frank McGarth?
Did he kill Pa?"

"Frank was in Fort Davis at the time." Will pursed
his lips and shrugged helplessly. "But if I was a betting
man, I'd wager Frank was behind it, even if his finger
wasn't on the trigger."

"Jace went through the motions of looking for the
murderer, but that was all it was—the motions," Ann said.
"Some would even say Jace had a hand in the shooting,
but there was no one who could prove anything."

"It doesn't make sense," Wade said, shaking his head.
"Why would Hap and Sims stay with Frank after all of
this? Why would they sell the farm to Frank?"

Will stared at Wade. "Because your brothers didn't
know what was happening in Waco. They were in Fort
Davis."

Ann reached out and touched the back of Wade's
right hand. "There's more. I'm sorry, but Hap . . . Hap's
been killed. And from what Will has told me, Sims isn't
much better off, all crippled up the way he is."

Wade's gaze shifted between the husband and wife.
He felt as lost as he had back in Waco. His father had
been murdered; Hap was dead; Sims was now a cripple.
The bombardment of disasters came too fast for him to
comprehend. A numbness suffused his body and brain. In
spite of the dazed cloud crowding his head, he heard
himself ask, "How did Hap die? And what happened to
Sims?"

"The telling will take some time." Will motioned for
Ann to pour fresh coffee all around. "You have to understand how it was."

"I've got all night, if that's what it takes," Wade
answered, hate tingeing his voice.

"It was the promise of quick riches that got me to ride
with Frank, same as Hap and Sims," Will began. "There
was some money at the beginning, but never as much as

Frank had promised. Still, it was better than what we could make behind a plow back in Waco."

At first McGarth's cattle and horse operation had been strictly aboveboard, Will explained. Stock was purchased in south Texas and in Mexico, then driven to Jefferson and sold. The money was used to buy more horses and cows. That much Wade and Roy had already heard from Jace.

"As the herds became larger," Will continued, "Frank began to hire border drifters as hands. Shortly after that, rustled stock from both sides of the Rio Grande began showing up in Frank's herds."

Will paused and took a deep drink from his cup. "Hap and Sims got wind of what Frank and his border trash were up to. I guess the rest of us had a good idea that rustling had become Frank's main business, but we all looked the other way. Not Hap and Sims. They were getting ready to turn Frank in to the Texas Rangers. About that time Frank assigned them the task of watching over a hundred head of mustangs just up from Mexico.

"On the first night with those horses, a Comanche raiding party struck the herd, stampeding it through your brothers' camp. Hap was killed, and Sims was crippled when the mustangs broke both his legs and arms. I never saw a man so broken up as Sims was."

Will paused again, this time to draw in a breath and exhale it in a gust. "The funny thing was that the tracks showed that every one of the Comanches' ponies was shod. I never knew a Comanche to make use of a blacksmith."

Neither did Wade. Comanches rode unshod mustangs. It was more than obvious that Frank McGarth was behind Hap's death. "Where's Sims now?"

"Last time I saw him, he was still in Fort Davis," Will said. "He wasn't much use to himself or anyone else, 'cause he was hiding inside a whiskey bottle. Not that I blame him. Crippled the way he is, he has to be hurting more than most men could suffer in ten lifetimes."

Will reached over and took Ann's hand. "After what happened to your brothers, me and the others that originally went down to Fort Davis with Frank pulled out. We figured it wouldn't be too long before Frank decided we were in the way, too."

Wade pushed from the table. Piece after ugly piece fell together to a form a picture of treachery and murder. The moment he had heard Frank McGarth's name he should have known what to expect. Yet he had hoped for—

"Where ya goin'?" Roy's question to Wade was insistent.

Wade stopped by the kitchen, unaware he had walked across the room. He glanced back at Roy. "To the stage office. I've got a lot to think over."

"Tom Wright, you be careful." This from Ann, who stared at him with furrows of concern creasing her forehead. "It's Waco that Frank is after. He's just waiting for things to quiet down, now that the war's over; then he intends to move back and set up his own empire. He knows that when Texas starts growing again, it'll be in the eastern part of the state, not out west. He'll kill anyone who gets in his way."

"Unless someone kills him first." Wade's voice came flat and cold, devoid of emotion. He turned and walked from the house into the night.

Walking under the stars, Wade reflected that Ann was right: Frank McGarth was a dangerous man. As a boy of nineteen, Wade had learned that lesson. The same lesson had cost Hap his life and left Sims with little more than life. Ann had also been correct in assuming what he intended to do. There was only one way to deal with a man like Frank McGarth—kill him!

The crunch of sand and stone beneath boots penetrated Wade's thoughts. Someone was following him! With his hand on the Army Colt in his belt, he swirled around.

Roy stood there, blinking at his friend. "You ain't intendin' to shoot me, are you?"

Wade's fingers slipped from the pistol. "There's no need for you to come with me. You wanted to find Ann, and you've found her. What waits ahead in Fort Davis is no concern of yours."

Roy sucked at his teeth and shook his head. "I reckon I'll be the one to decide what concerns me or not. The way I see it, I hired on to ride shotgun for Mr. Gaynes, all the way to El Paso, and that's what I aim to do. Besides, it's the only job I've got at the moment."

Matthew Thacker moved along past the rows of headstones in the Austin graveyard, finally reaching a recent grave marked by a simple granite cross. He read the name engraved in the stone and the dates chiseled beneath. The numerals indicating the short span of years that had been the life of Clara Wheatley Thacker gave no hint of the love and joy she had crowded into that brief time, nor did the stonecutter's chisel make mention of the empty place her death had left in the life of the man who had loved her.

Thacker knelt beside the grave and bowed his head. The prayer he whispered was simple, one that his mother had taught him as a boy. He remembered that it was one of the psalms of David, but he could not recall which one. The Psalms had been his mother's favorite book of the bible. She often said that she could hear the music behind the words.

Before rising, Thacker placed a small bouquet of flowers at the center of the grave. These had been Clara's favorites—richly colored Texas bluebonnets. Not even the rosebushes he had brought to her from New Orleans on their first anniversary had meant as much to her as these wildflowers that grew throughout the state.

He rose, turned, and walked from the cemetery. As he had done for two days, he moved numbly through Austin's streets, heedless of those he passed. At home he found an unopened bottle of bourbon on the mantel. After leaving Charlie and Bess on the night of his return, he had purchased five such quart containers. The other four, now empty, were scattered in disarray around the chair he sank into. Tomorrow he would have to buy more, but for today he had this one.

The lack of a left hand did not prohibit his opening that bottle. He used his teeth to pull out the cork and then spat it aside. There would be no need to recork the bourbon: He would not stop till it was gone.

He lifted it to toast the empty house around him: "Till death do us part." He wait for the house to offer its own toast in reply. There was only silence. Thacker shook his head and shrugged. "Be that way, if you want. But you won't get your share of this."

He put the bottle to his lips and gulped three deep swallows. A sigh pushed from his chest as the liquor's warmth ran down his throat into his stomach. It was a good beginning, but it was not enough. He no longer sought mere numbness; it was oblivion he wanted.

He raised the container once more. This time no bitter words came in toast. He shrugged again and drained three more swallows of bourbon.

"Enjoying your self-pity, aren't you?"

Thacker's head lolled to the right. Charlie Powell stood in the parlor doorway. "Pull off a sheet and have a seat. But if you'd like a drink, you'd better get your own bottle. This one belongs to me." Thacker took another swig of the amber liquid.

Charlie shook his head in disgust. "This isn't the Matthew Thacker I know. How do you expect Clara would feel to know you're turning yourself into a common drunk?"

"She can't feel anything," Thacker replied. "She's dead, remember?"

"As good an excuse as any, I suppose, to throw away the rest of your life." Abhorrence brimmed in Charlie's tone.

"It's my life." Thacker punctuated his remark with another slug of whiskey.

"What about David? Doesn't your life belong to him in part?" Charlie demanded. "Do you intend to leave him with your sister in Fort Stockton?"

David? Thacker hesitated as he lifted the bottle to his lips. He had avoided thinking about his son ever since Charlie and his wife had told him about Vera's taking the boy to Fort Stockton. His sister's intent, he had been told, was to look after David until Thacker returned home.

"Weren't you listening when Bess and I said your

sister had taken David with her the very day you came home? They were with us until it was time to go to the stagecoach." Charlie refused to stop. "We knew you couldn't go after David right away—you needed time to absorb the loss of Clara. But he's your son, Matthew. A seven-year-old boy! If Clara's memory means nothing to you, if you don't care anything about yourself, then think of the boy. Good lord, man, the boy needs a strong father—not a town drunk!"

Thacker winced. Charlie struck too close to home. A drunken stupor was exactly where he wanted to spend his life. That was until Charlie had mentioned David. His friend was right; David *was* his son. More important, David was *Clara's* son!

"You can't live like this," Charlie's voice droned on. "You have to think of your son. If you can't be a man for yourself, then be one for him."

Thacker's gaze lowered to the bottle in his hand. "You're right, Charlie." Without batting an eye, he sent the container hurling across the room, shattering it against the wall. He watched the liquor cascade down the rose-patterned wallpaper, a scene reminiscent of a hotel room in Waco. Only this time, he promised himself, there would be no more bourbon.

He rose abruptly from his chair, his legs surprisingly steady for the amount of alcohol he had consumed. "I'm going after David. A son belongs with his father."

And he would do this just as soon as he had taken the time to pull himself together and collect on an old promise.

Chapter Seven

Zach Farris, white sleeves rolled to the elbows and black vest unbuttoned, walked from his office out into the dusty street. As Ramsey Gaynes's San Antonio office manager, he was known for his obsession with punctuality. Placing his hands on his hips, he rocked from heel to toe three times as he stared up the street. Unsatisfied with what he saw—or failed to see—he reached into his vest pocket and removed a gold watch, complete with chain and dove-shaped fob. Opening it, he gazed at the face for several seconds, and then snapped the cover closed. Rocking back and forth three more times, he pivoted on the balls of his feet and disappeared back into the office.

"Twelve noon on the dot is the way I make it." Roy glanced at Wade. "Zach there is better than a Swiss pocket watch."

Wade smiled in agreement. Since seven that morning Roy and he had sat outside the stagecoach office, waiting. Like clockwork the office manager had performed the same ritual every half hour.

Wade's own gaze ran up and down the street. The army gold and the escort, which originally had been due to arrive last night, had not shown up yet. The army had wired from Victoria yesterday that the contingent was running behind schedule and would not reach San Antonio until after noon today.

"Looks like we got a choice of sittin' here listenin' to the flies buzz or strollin' down to the boardin' house and seein' what's for dinner." Roy's eyes darted around as he tried to follow the flight of a nearby horsefly.

Wade started to correct his friend and then caught himself. He had been gone from Texas long enough to forget that Texans usually referred to the noonday meal as dinner rather than lunch. The evening meal was supper. "Roy, when you put it that way," Wade replied, "I'll take dinner. Besides, our passengers might like to know what's going on."

In unison the two men pushed from their chairs and started toward the river and the two-story boardinghouse, where the passengers had gathered to wait until the stage's departure.

As they walked, Wade lifted his eyes to the sky overhead. He silently cursed, unable to contain his frustration. A clear day like this should have brought him miles closer to Fort Davis and Frank McGarth. Instead, half a day had already been wasted while he sat idly on his hindquarters.

"It's kinda interestin'," Roy said, "to find out that the Yankees can't keep to a schedule any better'n our army could. For a while there, I was thinkin' that the way our generals kept makin' us hurry up and wait was the reason we lost the war."

Wade did not comment. The war was behind him now; it served no purpose to dwell on it. Fort Davis lay ahead of him. There, one final battle awaited him.

"Hmm-*hmm*! Just take a whiff of that." Roy halted and sucked in a deep breath through his nostrils as they reached the two steps that led up to the porch of the boardinghouse. "That's fried chicken for sure. Biscuits, gravy, and corn on the cob, too, unless I miss my bet."

Testing the air, Wade detected the aroma of fried chicken, but he was less certain about the other items on the menu. Nor did he particularly care: He would have no complaints if the boardinghouse served nothing else but fried chicken. On the long hungry road from Virginia, he had learned not to be particular, and just one drumstick would have constituted a banquet—

"Please, no! I wouldn't care for any. I don't drink strong spirits."

Wade's head snapped around. The voice was unmistakably Laura Parvin's, and her tone conveyed acute distress. The young woman was to his right; she sat alone on a porch swing, and the source of her annoyance was an unshaven man who held a bottle out to her.

"It won't hurt you none to try bein' nice, ma'am. This ain't poison or nothin'." Deke Harris, one of the stagecoach passengers, thrust the bottle in Laura's face. "It's tequila. Just a li'l ol' cactus juice." He lifted the container and took a swig. "See there? It ain't gonna hurt you none. It just burns a little goin' down."

"Please, Mr. Harris. I really would not care to sample your tequila." Laura edged sideways along the swing and tried to rise.

Harris was blocking her. "Just one little sip. How you know you don't like it if you ain't tried it?"

In a single stride, Wade leapt to the porch. Another three strides brought him to Harris's side. Grasping the man's shoulder, he gently pulled Harris aside and held out a hand to help Laura from the swing.

"Hey, what—?" Harris turned and blinked several times, as if trying to focus on Wade's face. Although his words were not slurred, there was a thick-tongued sound to them that said Harris had been using the tequila to help pass the time until the stagecoach left San Antonio. He squinted at Wade resentfully. "Look here, stage driver, whaddya think you're doin'?"

"Miss Parvin said she didn't care for a drink." Wade held himself in check. After all, Harris was a paying customer, and Laura was unharmed. He glanced at the young woman, his hand still extended. "Why don't you go inside, Miss Parvin? I believe lunch is ready."

"What are you tryin' to do?" Harris's arm shot out, slapping Wade's hand away from Laura. "This ain't no concern of yours. You ain't nothin' but the hired help. Go back to your horses and leave me and this young lady alone. Ain't neither one of us need you stickin' your nose into our affairs."

"Thank you for your assistance, Mr. Bonner. I'd be honored if you'd accompany me for lunch." Before Wade could answer, Laura reached out and took his hand.

It was more than obvious to Wade that Laura was trying politely to ignore Harris's rudeness, in order to avert a confrontation. Her desire apparently was not as obvious to Harris.

"I *said* this ain't no concern of yours, driver! And I damned well meant it!"

Harris's arm snaked out again. This time his fingers clamped into Wade's shoulder and locked there, jerking Wade around to face him. Simultaneously, Harris slammed his left fist into Wade's stomach.

Wade groaned, the air driven from his lungs by the unexpected blow. In an involuntary response, he grabbed at his stomach as his body doubled over. Before he could recover, Harris struck again, his right fist hammering into the left side of Wade's face. Unable to maintain his footing, Wade went down sprawling on the porch.

"I told you to butt out." Harris loomed over him. "Now maybe you've learned I mean what I say." He took another swig from the bottle of tequila and grinned with delight.

Wade shook his head to fight off the shooting stars exploding in it and the throbbing pain that lanced along his right jaw. Pushing to an elbow, he stared up; his vision cleared to a watery blur. For the first time he realized how big Harris was. The man stood at least three inches above Wade's own height and appeared twice as wide.

"I wouldn't get up from there if I was you." Harris's tone almost begged Wade to rise again.

My first mistake was thinking he was drunk, Wade told himself as he started to rise, all the while hoping he was not making his second mistake by trying to pick himself up.

He was.

"I warned you!" Harris's right foot lashed out as Wade pushed himself to a crouch.

There was no time to dodge the pointed toe of Harris's boot. Wade's arms provided his only defense as he swung them up to absorb the brunt of Harris's attack. The impact sent Wade tumbling back in a head-over-heels somersault across the wooden porch.

Scrambling to right himself, Wade regained his footing just as Harris charged forward with arms thrown wide, ready to ensare his victim.

Wade quelled the urge to leap aside. Instead he crouched where he stood, muscles tensed like coiled springs, measuring the rapidly closing distance between Harris and himself. With Harris a single stride away, Wade sprang forward. His right shoulder buried itself in the man's gut, lifting him from the porch.

From there the battle was a matter of simple leverage. Harris's size and momentum worked against him. Wade pushed straight up and with a thrust of his hands sent the larger man sailing over his head. Harris's arms and legs were flailing as he flipped in midair before crashing down to the unyielding porch, back first.

Wade spun around. The advantage now his, he refused to relinquish it. As Harris rolled to his stomach and pushed to his knees, Wade stepped forward, and with the full weight of his body behind his blow, he connected a solidly thrown uppercut to Harris's chin.

The man's head snapped back, his eyes rolling in his head. For the space of three heartbeats he teetered on his knees, swaying from side to side. Then he fell, collapsing facedown on the white-painted boards.

Chest heaving and fists clenched in readiness for a renewed attack, Wade stood glaring down at the unmoving man.

"Are you all right?"

Laura's voice and the gentle touch of her hand on his shoulder convinced him that it was over. The fight was out of Harris, at least until he woke up.

"I'm okay." Wade nodded as he released the breath he had been holding.

"There's blood on your mouth." She took a lacy handkerchief from a handbag and dabbed at the corner of his lips.

Roy moved close to his friend and examined both sides of his face, as though appraising the damage Harris's fist had wrought. "It ain't nothin', ma'am. Just a little

scratch from a lucky punch. Wade here wasn't doin' nothin'
'cept workin' up an appetite for dinner."

Wade groaned inwardly. Roy's levity might be reassuring to Laura, but all it said to Wade was that Roy had
not felt the impact of Harris's fists. The man's blows had
had the force of a mule's kick behind them, and if the
pains in Wade's stomach and jaw were any indication, he
would not be able to look at food for a day or more, let
alone eat it.

Roy glanced toward the street, and a curse slipped
from his lips. "Don't look like that appetite's gonna do you
a bit of good, Wade."

Wade's head lifted, and he followed his friend's gaze.
Six soldiers in blue uniforms with shiny brass buttons
stood outside the stagecoach office, talking with Zach Farris.
Wade frowned. The soldiers were expected, but what was
unexpected were the two road wagons that stood on the
street. The bed of each wagon was covered with a heavy
tarpaulin.

"Roy, you and Miss Parvin go ahead and eat. I'll
check this out." Wade stepped from the porch.

"What about him?" Roy called out, nodding to the
unconscious Harris.

Wade glanced over his shoulder. "If he hasn't come
to by the time you're through eating, toss a bucket of
water on him." He waved off comment, turned, and headed
down the street.

Halfway to the office, Zach Farris lifted an arm to
signal him to hurry. With his body still aching from Harris's punishing blows, a trot was the best Wade could
manage.

"—let me talk with him," he heard Zach Farris telling
a young lieutenant with razor-edged creases in his trousers. "I know this isn't what Mr. Gaynes told him to
expect."

"We'll both explain the change in plans," the officer
replied. "I can't see how it will prove an inconvenience."

"Inconvenience? Change in plans?" Wade queried as
he joined the two men. He looked at the road wagons and
then at the lieutenant. The man looked young, perhaps a

year or two younger than Wade's own twenty-four years. Not good for rough service on the Texas frontier. Worse, he was probably new: Men who had seen action during the war would not be concerned with creases in their trousers or mirror-polished boots such as this officer wore.

"The changes are minor," the lieutenant said before Zach could utter a syllable. Then he turned to Wade. "I'm Lieutenant G. Wesley Chase, and my orders are to tell you that you will be carrying the payroll gold for Fort Stockton as planned. The only difference is that the escort my men and I will provide will be riding in those wagons there rather than on horseback."

Wade did not answer, but walked to one of the road wagons. He untied a corner of the tarpaulin and tossed it back. His jaw sagged as he stared at the black letters stenciled across two yellow pine boxes. "Rifles?" he asked. "Are both these wagons filled with rifles?"

Zach nodded. "Rifles—and ammunition."

"What?" Wade stared at Chase, watching him nod in affirmation. "You can't be serious. I'm driving a stagecoach, not ramrodding an army wagon train."

"Gaynes Stagecoach Line is contracted to deliver a strongbox of army gold to Fort Stockton—under army escort. We're that escort," the lieutenant said, his back stiffening like a rail. "I don't believe you have a choice in this matter."

Wade's eyes narrowed. He felt himself beginning to dislike Lieutenant G. Wesley Chase. "Six men to help guard a strongbox *and* these two wagons? Why don't we just paint a big red, white, and blue sign and nail it on the stagecoach to tell the world that we're carrying valuables? It couldn't be more obvious than the wagons."

The lieutenant showed no sign of relaxing. "My men and I should be more than sufficient to protect the shipment. Army intelligence indicates that if we encounter any resistance, it will come from unorganized riffraff returning from the war who still haven't got it through their heads that the Confederate Army has been defeated."

Wade realized that he was wrong: It was not dislike he felt mounting inside him; it was hate. He had met more than one wet-behind-the-ears lieutenant during the war. Their arrogant attitudes and lack of experience could be easily tallied by the dead in their commands. "That 'unorganized riffraff,' Lieutenant, had the Union Army ducking and running for the better part of four years. If a couple of Texas boys take it into their heads to come after this gold, it won't be hard for them to get rid of you and your men. That's ammunition in those crates, Lieutenant. You'll be riding on top of powder kegs. One well-placed shot will be all that's needed to blow those wagons to kingdom come."

Lieutenant Chase's eyes widened as though that possibility had never occurred to him. The five soldiers standing beside the wagons shifted restlessly, their gazes nervously darting to the wagons they had been assigned to guard.

Zach spoke before the officer could answer. "Wagons or not, Wade, Lieutenant Chase is right. We're under contract to deliver the gold to Fort Stockton. We got to do like the army says."

Wade's lips parted, but he held back the string of curses that danced on his tongue. Like it or not, the decision was not his to make. He was only a stagecoach driver. He glanced at the heavily laden wagons and shook his head. They were certain to slow him down as the miles between way stations grew longer and the terrain to the west grew more rugged. But there was nothing he could do about it.

"I'll have the stage brought around to the office," Zach said. "Why don't you go down to the boardinghouse and gather up the passengers? It's time to be moving out. There's been too much of a delay as it is."

Wade acquiesced with a curt nod, turned, and headed for the boardinghouse.

Fifteen minutes later the passengers were lined up, ready to board the stage. Wade surveyed the now-familiar faces: Laura, Vera Brown, and her nephew, David; also the windmill salesman, Howard Dalrymple. The only newcomer was a man listed as Patrick Cliff, a passenger for El Paso. The man's boots and hat pegged him as a rancher or farmer, and from the way Howard Dalrymple was bending his ear, the salesman had sized Cliff up as a prospective client.

The final passenger, Deke Harris, was not in the line to board. Wade glanced around, finding the man standing at the rear of the coach beside Roy. His clothing still dripped water. Wade smiled; he had seen Roy take great pleasure in dousing the man with a bucket of cold spring water. Wade walked over to Harris.

"If you want to continue with this stage, Harris, I want it understood that you'll cause no more problems with the other passengers, especially the womenfolk," Wade said. "If that doesn't suit you, you can wait for the next stage."

"You'll get no more trouble from me." Harris glanced at his feet and nodded sheepishly. "I didn't mean nothin' earlier. It was just the likker talkin'."

Wade eyed the man, weighing the risk of allowing him back on the stage. The bruise on his chin, now turning purple, would give him second thoughts about throwing another punch in Wade's direction. "You can ride up top, as you did when we left Waco."

Harris's head jerked up. A hint of fiery anger flashed in his eyes for a heartbeat. "But I don't feel so good now, and there's room inside the coach."

"Up top," Wade repeated, "until you've had time to dry out."

For an instant, he thought the man intended to protest further. Instead Harris merely nodded and climbed to the stagecoach's roof.

Wade looked back at the two army road wagons lined up behind the Concord and shouted, "Okay, Lieutenant, let's move 'em out!"

Captain Jess Koop grasped Matthew Thacker's extended hand with both of his and shook it vigorously. "My God! Matt Thacker! I didn't think I'd ever see your ugly face again. Come on inside and let me take a good look at you."

Thacker followed Koop into the Texas Ranger headquarters in Austin. His old friend's office had one window, from which the capitol building was visible. The Ranger captain waved Thacker to a chair while he propped himself against the front of his desk, his arms folded.

"It's really good to see you, Matt." A pleased grin beamed from the older man's face. "A few of those in my old command didn't make it, you know. Will Bartley died in Tennessee, Cal Hanks in Georgia, Jim Cutler in Kentucky." He paused and shook his head. "A lot of old friends wearing both blue and gray have been lost."

Sorrow seemed to bend Koop down with an invisible weight. Thacker wanted to reach out and grasp his friend's arm in comfort, but nothing would have been more embarrassing to the man, so Thacker sat still.

The years that had passed since they had last met in this office had left traces of their passage on the captain. What had been crow's-feet radiating from the corners of Koop's eyes were now deep, fissurelike cracks in skin as tough as leather. Silver hair had turned snow white. Yet in spite of time's handprints, Jesse Koop had a strength that Thacker had seen in few men, even in the generals who had commanded the Union Army. He was a Texas Ranger in the finest tradition.

Koop glanced out the window, as if for an instant he were looking back into the past; then he turned to face Thacker. "You didn't come here to talk about old friends, did you, Matt? How can I help you?"

Thacker went directly to the heart of the matter. "I want back in the Rangers, Captain. You said that I should look you up after I returned. Now I'm here."

Koop nodded. "I don't see any problem there. The Rangers are changing and growing. We need men, especially here in Austin." He pointed out the window. "A lot of what we have to do will take place right over there in the capitol. We need men who can talk our language to all those lawyers who call themselves representatives and senators. If the Rangers are going to do their job the way it's supposed to be done, we need funding. The only way—"

"I want my *old* job back, Jess," Thacker interrupted

his friend. "I'm not cut out for riding herd over some desk; I never have been. I'm a Ranger."

A shadow darkened the man's expression when his gaze shifted back to Thacker. Koop made no pretense of concealing the direction of that gaze. Thacker had to make a conscious effort not to reach across and rub his left arm.

"Don't you want to reconsider that, Matt?" Koop now stared down at the floor.

"I'd like my old job back," Thacker repeated. "It's what I know—all I've ever been trained for."

"You aren't too old to learn other ways," Koop countered. "I've had to learn them. They're what's needed now."

Thacker shook his head. "Not for me. I want to be put where I can do some good. I don't care where you station me, just as long as I'm doing what I can do."

The Ranger captain's eyes returned to the window. For seconds he stared outside while he rubbed a hand over his neck. "Matt, look, you've only got one arm. You know I can't—"

"I can still handle a pistol." Thacker refused to let him finish. "I've trained myself to use a rifle again, my eye's as sharp as ever, and I can still ride a horse."

Koop listened, but he did not comment.

"It doesn't take two hands to track a man, Jess. And I've still got a good pair of eyes. White man or red, I was the best tracker you ever had ride with you."

"Matt, it's not your tracking ability I'm questioning." He reached down to his desk, lifted a handful of papers, and tossed them into Thacker's lap. "Take a look at those, Matt. Those are wanted men, and each and every one of those whoresons has two hands. Most of them could kill you ten different ways with either hand. I'd never send a man with one arm after any of those dogs. You know why?"

Koop did not give him the chance to answer. "I'll tell you why—because I like to see my men come back alive. I don't care whether they bring back their prisoners dead or alive, so long as they keep *themselves* alive. It's that simple. There's nothing else to it."

Thacker stared at the wanted posters scattered over his lap and knees, and then he looked up at the Ranger captain. "I think you've made your position clear enough, Jess. I guess there's only one way to prove that this doesn't matter." He held up the pinned sleeve of coat. "Pick your man—any one of these—and I'll bring him back. It's that simple. There's nothing else to it." He grinned sardonically.

Koop winced, obviously irritated to hear his own words thrown back at him. "Don't be a jackass, Matt. I'm not trying to test you. I'm offering you a good job. Most of the men in this state would leap at the chance to get it."

Thacker scooped up the wanted posters with his right hand. "I've got myself a job right here, Koop. A hundred dollars, two, as much as a thousand for each of these men I bring in."

"A bounty hunter?" Koop stared at him in disbelief. "Now you're talking like a crazy man, Matt."

Stuffing the posters in a pocket, Thacker rose from the chair. "It's a way of making a living."

"So is working here in Austin."

"But it's not *my* way." Thacker tipped his hat, walked from the office, and left the headquarters.

Outside, the fresh Texas air did nothing to quell the hammering of his heart. He should have been prepared for the captain's reaction, but he had not been. His strides quickened as he moved down the street toward a small park at the center of the town. If he doubted himself, why had he not seen that others would doubt his ability? The only way was to show them that he was still the man he had once been—to show Koop.

And himself?

That was more than half of it, he realized as he found a park bench and sank onto it. How could Koop believe in him, if he himself did not? And there *was* doubt; he could not escape that.

He tugged the crumpled handbills from his pocket, placed them on the bench beside him and began to shuffle through them. Bounty hunting was not the life he was seeking, but if bringing in one of these men was what it would take to convince Koop he was still the man he had once been . . .

Thacker paused suddenly, his thoughts racing. He shifted back through the posters. There! He had almost overlooked it because the reward offered was only seventy-five dollars. Leaning back, he held the handbill out at arm's length, studying the line drawing on it. Mentally he drew a dark-brown beard over the clean-shaven cheeks portrayed in the poster. *My God, it's him! How could I have forgotten him?*

He did not need to read the name that was printed in bold print beneath the words Wanted For Murder. The name was Tom Wright—Tom Wright, the only man Thacker had ever let escape from custody. How had he ever forgotten him?

A groan worked up from his throat. It was Wright who had driven the stage that had brought him to Austin! And from what Charlie had told him, he knew it was the same stagecoach that was now carrying his son and sister westward toward Fort Stockton. And the driver had told him he was staying with the coach all the way to El Paso!

Leaving the rest of the posters on the bench, Thacker carefully folded the one bearing Tom Wright's picture and slipped it back into a pocket as he stood up. He needed to look no further for a man to hunt down; fate had dealt him an unexpected hole card, one he planned to play.

Determination guided Thacker's feet as he strode from the park. He needed a good horse, tack, and supplies before he could ride west after his son and after a killer who had escaped him five years ago.

Chapter Eight

"**Y**ou're lucky you caught this." The blacksmith glanced up at Wade Bonner from where he squatted beside the stagecoach's left rear wheel. "You wouldn't have gotten more'n five miles on this rim before it broke all the way through on you. Then where'd you be?"

The severity of the problem was apparent to Wade. When he had noticed the widening crack in the wheel's iron rim—back at the last way station—he had not been certain the wheel would last the fifteen miles needed to reach Kerrville. Luckily it had held.

"Must have been one big rock you hit to cause this." The blacksmith shook his head as he stood. "The rim doesn't look old."

Wade honestly could not recall which rock or pothole in the road was responsible for the cracked rim. All he remembered was feeling an unnatural vibration running through the stagecoach, which had made him double-check the wheels at the last way station. "How long will it take for you to fix it?"

The blacksmith rubbed the back of his bull-like neck. "The wheel will have to come off 'fore I can remove the rim. The forge is already fired up, so that'll save some time." He looked at Wade. "Three hours—maybe two, if I get right at it."

Wade did not argue but gave the man the go-ahead to start the repairs. Kerrville was not a major stop, and the schedule allowed no more time there than was needed to change horses and load new passengers. This new delay was the last thing he wanted: The stage already was travel-

91

ing at a snail's pace, thanks to Lieutenant Chase and his road wagons. Wade's eyes lifted to the west. In spite of the miles that lay behind, Fort Davis seemed as distant as ever.

"Is it that bad?"

Wade turned. Laura Parvin stood there staring at the stagecoach. Her emerald eyes rose to his. "Roy's been telling the passengers at the station that it's only a minor problem, but from the look on your face, I'd say we've encountered a disaster."

A smile slid across Wade's lips. "I'm a natural-born worrier. Shouldn't take more than three hours to fix this wheel."

"Then there's time for you to eat." Laura held up a small wicker basket. "I borrowed this from Mrs. Wharton at the station. She packed it with a couple of ham sandwiches, two hardboiled eggs, and a jar of water. I thought you might enjoy a picnic."

"Picnic?" Wade grinned as he gave the dusty little town a hasty survey. "Here?"

Laura pointed to three large trees that grew a hundred yards north of the way station. "It looks grassy and shady over there—just the right spot to enjoy a bit of lunch."

Wade waved a hand for her to lead the way, tactfully not mentioning the fact that the wind-twisted trees Laura had selected as shelter from the midday Texas sun were mesquites. Mesquites, with their small leaves, had a way of promising shade and lying. But neither Laura nor Wade seemed to mind the sun as they settled themselves beneath a tree on a patch of buffalo grass.

Laura's gaze moved over the land surrounding them. "It's hard to believe that this is the same state I entered back in Texarkana. Back there I saw nothing but pine trees and hills. Out here it's—"

"Rocks and lizards," Wade finished for her. "I know what you mean. It's rough country."

"No, that's not what I was trying to say, although this part of Texas *is* rugged," she said as she peeled a hardboiled egg and passed it to him. "I don't know exactly why, but I really enjoy just watching the country."

"There's little to do inside the coach *except* watch the country roll by," Wade said. "As a matter of fact that's about all there is to do up in the driver's box."

"You're teasing me." Laura shyly glanced away, and for an instant Wade thought that he might have insulted her. He breathed a silent sigh of relief when she said, "I don't care, Wade Bonner. I may sound silly, but I'm fascinated by this land you call Texas. It seems to change its face with each new day."

He listened as she described all she had seen. What he had always taken as commonplace seemed, through Laura's eyes, to be reborn with a sense of wonder. Even a scrawny longhorn steer, wandering through the chaparral, was a thing of beauty when this young woman described it.

"There's more to Texas than what you've seen," he said while they finished their sandwiches. He spoke of the gulf coast with its white sand beaches and palm trees and bayous inhabited by alligators. "Even the country you see here, as rough as it looks, is good land. A man can make a living dry farming here. Fact is, most of Texas is ready-made for the plow or grazing stock."

"But the desert? My father has written about the desert," she said.

"You won't run into that until we're almost to El Paso." He described how the Chihuahuan desert swept northward out of Mexico into Texas and New Mexico Territory.

"And you want to settle in New Mexico?" Her eyebrows arched dubiously.

"Not in the desert, but maybe up north, around Santa Fe." Wade smiled to hide the lie. After returning to Texas it would be hard to leave his home again. *Damn hard*, he admitted to himself. "I want some land that I can work and maybe run a few head of cattle."

Laura's eyes lifted. For several moments, she stared into his gray eyes as though probing his soul. What did she see? What was she thinking? Was she wondering how many pretty faces with enticing smiles had turned his head? He had seen many during the war; like the endless string of towns and villages he had marched through, they were nameless in his mind. They had meant nothing to him, and he had always refused their unstated invitations. . . .

Laura was not one of those. Her emerald eyes and shy smile were like the petals of a unique blossom, inviting him to discover what lay behind them. To Wade's surprise, he wanted to know the thoughts that moved behind those eyes.

Laura broke the silence. "It's getting late. Shouldn't we be getting back to the others?"

He wanted to say no, that it would not matter if they sat beneath the mesquites until the sun settled behind the western horizon and the stars sprinkled the sky overhead. Instead he said, "I guess I should check on how that wheel's coming."

Laura rose to her knees and stretched toward Wade to collect the remains of their lunch from the grass. Without conscious thought, he also leaned forward. His mouth lightly brushed the warmth of her lips for a fleeting moment.

If he expected her to retreat suddenly, her shy gaze refusing to meet his, he was mistaken. Laura looked into his eyes, her head tilted slightly to one side, and then she leaned back to him. Their mouths met again, opening to one another.

Deke Harris stepped from the way station and picked at his teeth with a fingernail as he glanced up and down Kerrville's single street. The meal that filled his belly had been satisfying, even though it had been nothing more than prairie stew. The dollar price had been too steep, but stagecoach way stations always gouged passengers. At least it was not his own money he spent; Frank McGarth had been generous. But then there was good reason for the man's generosity.

Harris's gaze moved to the stagecoach and army wagons standing outside the town's livery stable. He smiled. McGarth had been right about the blue bellies' gold. However, the two road wagons filled with rifles and ammunition were an unexpected prize. They would bring a handsome profit below the Rio Grande.

Harris's smile widened. On second thought, the weapons might bring a prettier penny with the Comancheros up in New Mexico Territory. Not that disposing of the rifles and ammunition was his responsibility. That was McGarth's worry. Harris's sole concern was how to spend his share of the money that came from the sale.

And lettin' McGarth know where the stage and wagons are. That was the purpose of Harris's stagecoach journey, and it pushed to the forefront of his thoughts. Before he could spend his share of the money, McGarth and the boys had to take the strongbox and the wagons.

A small shingle hanging over a doorway fifty feet from the stable caught Harris's eye—the town's telegraph office. McGarth had told him to wire Fort Davis the moment the gold arrived in San Antonio. But there had not been time then, not after his run-in with the stage driver.

Harris's fingertips rose to his chin and gingerly brushed over the tenderness there. For a little man—little to Harris was anyone shorter than his own six feet two inches—the driver packed quite a wallop in his right fist. The swelling caused by Wade Bonner's blow was almost gone, but the purple bruise would persist for several weeks, as a humiliating reminder of the man's lucky punch. If it had not been for the tequila clouding his mind, Harris told himself, Bonner would never had laid a finger on him, let alone left him stretched out on the boardinghouse porch.

Harris's gaze moved down the sandy street to three mesquite trees growing beyond the last building. His eyes narrowed to slits as he caught sight of Wade and Laura seated there; then he saw them kiss, their fingertips lightly caressing each other's faces. *Well, I'll be—ain't that a pretty picture!* he thought. No wonder the feisty little driver had taken him on. The man wanted to keep that sweet-smelling filly all for himself!

The smile that twisted Harris's lips bore no trace of humor. When McGarth and the boys made their move outside Fort Stockton, he would have to show Wade Bonner that it did not pay to be greedy. Harris chuckled.

After he taught the driver a lesson, he had a few things he planned to teach that high-and-mighty Laura Parvin, and none of them had a thing to do with drinking tequila.

Enjoying his thoughts of pleasure to come, he walked into the telegraph office.

"Friend!" shouted a man in a bright green suit with a checkered vest. "You look like a man who could use a miracle or two. And that's what I'm here to sell you for one silver dollar. Doctor J. A. Sarrantonio's Miracle Elixir and Horse Liniment! Guaranteed to cure all the ailments of man—great or small!"

Matthew Thacker glanced at the snake-oil salesman who hawked his wares on a San Antonio street corner. He turned away without so much as a nod to acknowledge the man. The only results a man could expect from such an elixir, if he was foolish enough to drink a bottle, was a hangover—if he did not go blind first. Thacker had once looked into a traveling medicine show's mixing barrel. Rotgut was ninety percent of its contents; the rest was boot polish, nitric acid, peach pits, rattlesnake heads, and a few iron nails thrown in for flavor and coloring.

"Only one dollar, friend," the man's voice faded behind Thacker as he moved down San Antonio's streets.

Near the river, Thacker saw what he was searching for—the Gaynes Stagecoach Line office. He tapped his heels against the sides of the bay gelding he rode, quickening the horse's pace.

"Tarnation and perdition, Clem Barker! That hurt like all getout!"

Thacker turned to his right, and through the open door of a barbershop he saw a man clutch the right side of his jaw and then snatch a blood-spotted barber's bib from around his neck and jump from his chair.

The barber held out a pair of pliers to display a tooth. "Todd, you just calm down and stop actin' like a fool. I done pulled the thing that was causin' you the trouble. Now go get yourself a drink. It'll ease the pain a mite."

"One drink? It'll take a whole bottle to stop—"

Thacker shut the men's voices from his mind as he

drew the bay to a halt in front of the stage office. Swinging down from the saddle, he slipped the reins over his mount's head and tied them to the iron ring of a hitching post.

Inside the office a lone man sat behind a desk, reading a newspaper. A sign on his desk identified him as Zach Farris. Glancing up at Thacker, he asked, "How can I help you, friend?"

"I'd like some information about a woman and a boy who boarded one of your coaches in Austin," he answered. "The woman's name is Vera Brown, the boy's David Thacker. He's my son."

For a second Thacker considered the possibility of mentioning Ramsey Gaynes's name as a means of encouraging cooperation. There was no need; Farris set aside his newspaper as he began rummaging through a stack of papers piled on one side of the desk.

"Yeah, here it is. I thought I recalled that name." The man held up a yellow sheet of paper that he handed to Thacker. "Vera Brown, traveling with her nephew."

Thacker found his sister's name with the destination of Fort Stockton written beside it. "Are they still in town?"

"Not hardly." The stationmaster shook his head. "That stage pulled out of town two days ago. Traveling with an army escort it was."

"Army escort?" Thacker's brow knitted in question.

"Yep," Ferris said. "Six soldiers in road wagons are going along behind the stage. On their way to Fort Stockton. Rifles and ammunition on the wagons, and gold on the—" He stopped abruptly, as if realizing that he was telling too much to a stranger.

Thacker smiled. "Don't worry, mister. I'm not after either the guns or the gold. Your information is safe with me."

Farris looked relieved, and Thacker gave him another reassuring smile as he did some figuring. Wade Bonner would be hard pressed to make good time with those wagons dragging along. The stagecoach's two days' head start seemed shorter than it had a moment earlier.

"Is there a place in town a man can get a hot meal and maybe grab a couple of hours' sleep?"

"There's a boardinghouse just down the street." Farris tilted his head toward the right. "Food's good, and the widow who runs it keeps a quiet house."

Thanking the man, Thacker left the office. After something to eat and a nap of an hour or two, he'd head westward. With luck, he would catch up with the stage in three or four days at the most, thanks to the U.S. Army.

Chapter Nine

Giving the reins a single loop around the broad Mexican-style horn of his saddle, Thacker let the bay have its head while it picked its way over the rocky terrain among the ground-hugging clumps of dagger-spiked yucca that Texans called bear grass. Reaching across his chest with his right hand, he rubbed at his left arm through his shirt.

His breath hissed through clenched teeth. The pain in his arm came and went. For each hour's respite, there were three of a nagging throbbing that built in intensity until it could no longer be ignored. Maybe Captain Koop had been right. This was not a job for a man with only one—

No! Thacker shoved the thought from his mind. His lack of a left arm did not hinder him, and even without bourbon, he had been dealing with the pain. The tracks of the stagecoach that he was following were less than four hours old. He needed no other proof than this of his ability to handle the task he had set for himself.

Releasing his left arm, he reached around to massage the tight muscles at the small of his back. Although he had almost accomplished the goal he had set for himself four days ago in San Antonio, it had not come without a price. He had pushed himself, limiting the trail he covered only by the needs of his mount. He rested, ate, and slept when the bay required the same, never when his own body demanded it.

Thacker shifted his weight in the saddle. The movement did nothing to relieve the kinks in his back or the soreness of his buttocks and thighs. More than a year had

99

passed since he had last sat astride a horse—a fact that was
made more than evident by the aches and pains that
plagued every inch of his body.

Worse than the pain was the lack of sleep. Since
leaving San Antonio, the longest stretch of sleep he had
gotten was four hours two nights ago.

Stretch—the word rang with irony in his head, for the
one thing he wanted to do more than anything at this very
moment was to stretch out on a thick feather bed and
sleep for days and days.

A smile touched the corners of his mouth. Once such
a ride had been standard fare for him, but that had been
before the war. He had gone soft since then, forgetting
what it was like being on the trail of a man.

And this one does not even know that I am after him.
This fact, Thacker realized, explained the freshness of the
wheel tracks he leaned down to examine. If Tom Wright
had had any idea that a man holding a five-year-old wanted
poster was following him, he would doubtless have aban-
doned the stagecoach long ago in favor of a fast horse.

Wright was a slippery one; Thacker was only too
aware of that fact. No other man had ever managed to
escape him. Even now, Thacker was not certain just how
Wright had taken him that night outside Waco. All he
remembered was that he had been slipping handcuffs on a
frightened nineteen-year-old boy, and in the next instant
that boy had got hold of the Ranger's gun and was order-
ing him to hug a pine sapling while his own handcuffs
were snapped around his wrists.

Eight hours had passed before a farmer on his way
into Waco had discovered Thacker. Two additional hours
had been needed for a blacksmith to remove the cuffs.
Those ten hours had been more than enough time for
Wright to make good his escape. He had been smart,
Thacker recalled, covering his trail like a Comanche brave
fleeing a blood enemy. Ten miles north of Waco, Thacker
had lost Wright's trail completely, and he had returned to
Waco like some green deputy, without his man or a clue
as to where he had gone.

This time would be different, Thacker swore. This

time he held the advantage of surprise, and he intended to press it to the fullest. But it would be only when the time was right: Both his son and sister rode the stagecoach with Wright, and their safety came first—no matter how badly he wanted to drag Wright into Koop's office to prove that he could still handle a Ranger's job.

But he *did* have the advantage, and that was what was important. Wright had not recognized him while he had been on the stagecoach; of that, Thacker was certain. That meant he would be able to ride right up to the stage, remove Vera and David from danger, and then take Wright. A simple plan, but simple plans were always the best.

The bay's slowing strides drew Thacker out of his reflections. He unlooped the reins from the horn and pulled the gelding to a halt. The horse was growing tired again, and its rider did not begrudge the gelding that weariness: Four hours had passed since man or animal had rested.

Shifting his weight from one stirrup to the other, Thacker surveyed the land around him. A patch of green a quarter of a mile farther west drew his eye, and he identified it as a copse of black willow trees. His heels tapped the bay's sides, moving the horse forward. If luck rode on his shoulder, the willows sat beside a spring or water hole. At worst, the bushy trees would provide shade while he rested.

A spring had been too much to hope for, he realized, as he pulled up beside the gnarled willows and dismounted. The trees grew beside a dried creek bed. Their foliage told of recent spring rains, but the creek's sun-parched, sandy bed said those rains had come weeks earlier.

Thacker pulled one of two canteens from the saddle horn. From one of the saddlebags he scooped a double handful of oats and mounded the grain on the ground. The bay could eat oats and what sparse grass it could find while he rested. Before he mounted again, Thacker would water the horse from the remaining canteen. A leather hobble binding the animal's forelegs would assure that the gelding did not wander more than a few yards while its rider slept.

Walking around the horse, Thacker extracted a twist

of jerked venison from the opposite saddlebag. He glanced westward. The sun would be down in another half hour. Water and jerky were his fare tonight; he was unwilling to risk a campfire with the stage so near. Light, even the brief blaze of a match, could be seen for twenty miles in these flatlands after nightfall.

Eyes sharper than Tom Wright's watched the plains, Thacker thought as he settled beneath the stingy shade cast by the willows. *Comancheria* was the name the Spanish had given this land, and the Comanche was still lord of the plains. He closed his eyes. Comanches would be of no concern until after sunset, when their raiding parties rode across the plains. He would worry about them then. Now he needed to rest.

A cold breeze from the north washed over his face. Thacker smiled, his eyes opening. He blinked. The sky was dark! Diamond bright stars winked overhead!

He thrust up, supporting himself on his elbows. He had slept like a dead man, without dreams or knowledge of his act. How much time had gone by—two hours? Five?

Swinging around, he scanned the sky, picking out the familiar shapes of constellations. The backward question mark and attached triangle of stars that formed Leo the lion rode directly overhead. *Nine o'clock at the latest*. The realization calmed him: He had slept no more than three hours, an hour more than he had wanted, perhaps, but at least he had not slept through the whole night.

Nor had his mount wandered far. The gelding grazed on a clump of buffalo grass twenty yards to his left.

Thacker pushed up until he sat cross-legged on the ground. He looked at the jerky still clenched in his right hand and deposited the dried, peppery venison in a shirt pocket. There would be time to eat when he was in the saddle again. He allowed himself two mouthfuls of water from the canteen on the ground beside him before he stood.

Standing was a mistake; it awoke every ache and pain in his body. *You're getting old*, he tried to, kid himself as he walked toward the bay. The mental jest did nothing to improve his mood. It struck too close to home.

Thacker took off his hat, emptied the contents of the canteen into it, and allowed the bay to drink. Springs and water holes were few and far between in this country. The canteen still strung from the saddle horn would have to last the horse and him until he found water. When the bay had emptied the hat, he returned it to his head. The droplets that trickled down his neck and back felt good, for the night was hot and hours remained before the earth would give up the heat of the day.

Kneeling, he removed the hobble from the horse's forelegs and then rose to check the saddle's girth. Assured the cinch was tight enough, he stepped into a stirrup and rose to the saddle.

In the west, as the constellation of Gemini, the twins, rode above the horizon, Thacker spotted a yellow-orange glow of a campfire flickering in the southwest no more than a mile away. He frowned. No Comanche would be fool enough to light a fire at night in this country. Nor would a white man, if he wanted to keep his hair on his head and not dangling from some brave's tepee.

It's some fool farmer, he thought, as he nudged the bay forward with his heels. *Some greenhorn taking his family west and maybe getting them killed in the process.*

Thacker reined toward the beaconlike blaze. It was not just what Comanches would do to the man who had lit the fire that concerned him; it was what they would do to his family. All too often, during his years as a Ranger, he had seen the bloody remains of what had once been women and children, and he would intervene now to prevent an innocent and helpless family from being tortured and butchered because of their man's sheer stupidity.

A quarter of a mile from the campfire, Thacker drew up the bay. Furrows ran deep across his forehead as his eyes narrowed. This was no family camped for the night. Men, their bodies silhouetted by the bright flames, moved back and forth in front of the fire. At the periphery of the yellow-orange glow stood a remuda of ten or more horses.

Caution guided Thacker's movements as he eased from the saddle to the ground and tied the gelding's reins to a low-hanging mesquite branch. He immediately discarded his first thought that these men might be a Ranger company on patrol. Since the days of the Republic of Texas, Rangers had always cold-camped whenever they rode into Comanche territory. What were white men doing out in the middle of nowhere?

In a crouch, he eased from mesquite to brush to scrub tree, working to the edge of the campfire's ring of light and settling behind a bushy cedar. He pushed one of the needled branches aside, and his eyes widened in bewilderment as he stared at the camp twenty-five strides from his position.

Twenty men stood around the fire—all of them stripped down to longjohns and boots!

"All right, boys, get into them Reb uniforms." A man whose face Thacker could not discern shouted the command. "I want all of you to move out when I give the word."

"This ain't no uniform," another man returned. "It ain't nothing but dirty rags!"

The first answered, "It'll be all that's needed to make them army boys think they was hit by renegades when we take the stage at Sheffield Station. You ain't supposed to be duded up like you was about to go to Sunday meetin'."

"Frank's right, Cotton," another voice called out. "Just think about all that army gold that will be ours 'round about midnight!"

"After you're dressed"—the first man spoke again—"pack up your own duds; then eat and get what rest you can. Once we mount up, ain't none of us gonna be sleepin' the rest of this night."

Sweat prickled over Thacker's body in a cold chill that had nothing to do with the north wind. He did not need to hear more. These men, disguised as renegade Rebel soldiers, intended to rob the stagecoach. The six soldiers escorting the stage would not stand much of a chance against twenty. Even counting Wright, the shotgunner, and male passengers, the outlaw band outnumbered them two to one. Those odds might be acceptable in a horse race, but not in a fight.

Thacker sank back into the night. Foot by foot he

moved, carefully placing his boots so that neither a broken twig nor the crunch of rocks beneath his feet would give him away. Reaching the bay, he climbed back into the saddle. A brief glance back at the camp revealed that all remained quiet. He had gone undiscovered.

To the north, flashes of distant lightning lit the sky. He would ride in that direction for a mile before swinging westward and cutting south to Sheffield Station. Although it meant that he would have to reveal himself to Tom Wright, he had to warn the soldiers and the stagecoach of the impending midnight raid. His heels rose and fell, urging the bay northward.

Jagged bolts of lightning danced across the northern sky. From horizon to horizon the bolts seared the air. Behind the actinic glare of each flash that rent the night loomed dark thunderheads, boiling mountains in the sky that rolled over the plains

"Smell that air." Roy sucked in a deep breath through his nostrils. "There's rain in the wind. It's gonna come a frog strangler, just as sure as my name's J. Willis Henderson."

Wade laughed. "I didn't know you'd changed your name recently."

"I haven't." Roy gave his head an adamant shake. "But I'm cautious: I always use a false name when bettin' on the weather, 'cause I ain't ever been worth a damn when it comes to predictin' it."

Indeed, no forecast was worth much when it came to Texas weather, Wade reflected. The storm that was sweeping down from the north looked as if it would be a gully washer, but it was equally possible that the thunderheads now visible would abruptly slide off to the east or west, never coming far enough south to quench the thirst of this dry land.

Nevertheless, Wade, like Roy, would bet on rain tonight. Ahead he could see the Sheffield way station where the stage was scheduled for an hour's layover while the passengers had their evening meal. Sheets of rain would likely wash over the land before that meal was completed. The ride westward from the station toward Fort Stockton was going to be a wet one tonight.

"Wade, it don't look right up ahead." Roy reached over, nudged his friend, and pointed to the station. "I can't see no lights up yonder."

Wade frowned; Roy was right. A quarter of a mile separated them from the station. No lights came from the windows. There should be lights. The stage was expected.

Pulling back on the reins, Wade slowed the horses to a walk. It was a six-horse team, the third pair having been added in San Marcos. Wade slipped the Colt from his belt and cocked the hammer, while beside him Roy thumbed back the twin hammers of the shotgun he held.

The army wagons slowed too, and one of them, Lieutenant Chase aboard, came alongside. "What's up," Chase asked.

"Don't know yet," was Wade's laconic reply.

As the stagecoach and wagons rolled to a stop before the station, Roy shook his head. "It ain't lookin' good," he said. "It don't look like anybody's here."

Roy was giving voice to the obvious. Wade tugged back on the brake and lifted the Colt. "Wait here, Roy. You too, Lieutenant, and keep your men away. The stage and wagons will have to be covered, whatever happens. I'm going to take a look inside. If there's trouble, get the hell out of here and don't look back."

"You sure that's the way you want it?" Roy glanced at the dark way station. "My scattergun here can do a lot of damage in a short time, if it's needed."

"It's not the way I want it, but it's the way it has to be." Wade dropped to the ground.

"Young man," Vera Brown whispered as he moved around the stage, "is there a problem?"

Wade waved away her question and moved to the station's porch with his Colt leveled and ready. The creak of the porch's wooden boards beneath his boots sounded like the opening of rusty hinges. Why the sound seemed so alarming to his ears, he did not know. Anyone within the building was certain to know they had arrived; only a stone-deaf man could have missed the approach of the stagecoach.

With the fingers of his left hand, he reached out and touched the front door. It swung inward with no resistance. The reason—there was no one inside.

Wade stepped over the threshold. For several seconds he stood there, allowing his eyes to adjust to the interior darkness. Even through the dimness he could see the destruction. The station looked as if a tornado had ripped through it. Tables and chairs were turned over; windows were broken; dishes lay shattered on the floor.

Colt in hand, Wade moved through the building's main room to a bedroom belonging to the husband and wife who ran the station. Conditions here were just as bad: Blankets and sheets had been torn, and feathers from the shredded mattress were scattered everywhere, as though a snowstorm had struck this room.

"What is it?" Lieutenant Chase said as he entered the station.

"Thought I told you to stay back, Lieutenant," Wade replied with annoyance. "Well, I'm not sure what's happened." A candle on the floor near the bedroom door caught Wade's eye. Picking it up, he lit it. The way station looked twice as bad in the light.

"Comanches?" Chase asked.

"Could be." Wade could only guess who had wreaked this havoc, and guessing would do no good.

Whoever or whatever had hit the station had worked to the utmost to destroy every possession the owners kept in the two rooms. In the candle's glow he saw that the bed frame had been broken in three places. The ripped remnants of two dresses, one blue and another black with a white lace collar, were thrown about the bedroom. Among those frayed, ribbon-size pieces were scraps of a man's work shirt and breeches. Wade knelt and examined the rent fabric. The hand of man had been at work here. A knife blade had shredded the clothing.

"Bodies?" Chase found another candle and lit it from Wade's flame.

"Not that I saw." Wade stood. He found no trace of blood anywhere in the two rooms.

"The husband or wife might have taken sick," the lieutenant suggested. "They may have ridden into Fort Stockton to see the physician. Vandals could have broken into the station and done this."

"Could be," Wade replied with no trace of commitment in his tone. He was not certain where the young officer thought he was, but this was west Texas and not a city. Vandals did not lurk on every street corner in a land where the nearest neighbor was twenty miles away.

"What do you want to do?" Chase asked.

"Change teams and get out of here before whoever did this decides to come back," Wade replied. Something had gone wrong here, and he did not want anything like it to happen to the stagecoach. "Let your men and the passengers stretch their legs, but keep them by the coach and the wagons. There's no need for them to see this. Roy and I'll see about fresh horses."

Outside Wade waved his friend down from the driver's seat. Before the two could walk to the barn behind the station house, Howard Dalrymple called from the stage, "Driver, what's the matter? Is there something wrong?"

Wade turned back to the stagecoach. The heads of all his passengers poked out the windows. Worry was on their faces, even that of young David Thacker. "Just a little delay. That's all, folks. We'll be moving on as soon as we change teams."

"What about supper?" This from the boy. "Aunt Vera said we was gonna eat supper here."

"Supper'll have to wait until we reach the next station," Wade answered. "That isn't so far away. You can ride up top with Roy and me until we get there."

The boy agreed enthusiastically, although Vera Brown mumbled a few words of disapproval.

Wade heard Deke Harris start to say something, possibly to raise his own questions about the delay. He did not give the drifter a chance to finish, but instead turned and walked around the station toward the barn.

Roy followed him. "What's goin' on?" he demanded, eyeing his friend curiously.

"I'm not sure." Wade handed Roy the candle and then undid the latch on the barn doors, opened them, and stepped into the dark interior. "The whole house is torn up, but there's no sign of the man and woman who run this station."

"You're wrong about that, Tom."

Wade's head snapped around, and he looked sharply at Roy. "What makes you think—"

His words broke off as he saw the color draining from his friend's face; then he turned to see what Roy's candle was illuminating.

"My God!" Wade said. His stomach churned, threatening to upheave. They had found the husband and wife who ran Sheffield Station. "Get Lieutenant Chase."

"I think I'm gonna be sick, Wade." Roy clamped a hand over his mouth as though attempting to hold back his stomach.

"There isn't time for either of us to be sick." Wade forced his words to come with unwavering firmness. "Now go get the lieutenant."

Drawing in several steadying breaths, Roy nodded, passed the candle back to Wade, turned, and hurried away. It took Wade several silent moments to convince himself that there was a task to be done and he was the one who had to do it. A second look inside the barn did nothing to relieve the queasy knots that twisted his gut.

Too often he had seen what cannon and saber could do to a man, but the war had ill prepared him for the gruesome scene within the barn. The man and woman hung upside down from ropes strung over one of the rafters as if they were nothing more than sides of beef. Every inch of their naked bodies spoke of hours of agony before the final release of death. A fine-lined, deep-biting, crosshatched pattern covered their flesh. No draftsman's pen had drawn the crisscrossing design, but the blades of knives, methodically etching anguish with each slice of razor-honed steel. Death had mercifully come when those knives had been drawn across their throats.

Slipping his hunting knife from its sheath, Wade walked inside and severed the ropes holding the couple. Their bodies dropped heavily to the ground. To Wade it seemed like a final humiliation for a man and woman who had suffered far too much at the hands of their fellow man.

"Where are the horses, Bonner?" Lieutenant Chase demanded when he walked into the barn. "Why are you taking so—"

The young officer did not finish his sentence. Instead he pivoted, grasped his stomach, and doubled over. In the next moment his body was wracked with dry heaves.

Wade tried to find sympathy for the officer, but he could not. He was having enough trouble maintaining control over his own stomach. "There are no horses in here. And you won't find any outside in the corral. Comanches did this, and they don't leave any horses."

"Horses?" Chase straightened himself, wiping his mouth on a sleeve of his jacket. "What about horses?"

Wade shook his head. "There are none. Nothing is more important to a Comanche than horseflesh. That's why they hit this way station; they wanted the horses. And that's why they didn't burn this place to the ground. They want Ramsey Gaynes to send more people here with more horses so they can make another raid."

"No horses," Chase repeated as Wade's meaning penetrated. "We can't go on without fresh horses. It's been thirty miles since the last station, and our horses can't go on. They'll never make it to the next station."

"We'll do what we have to do," Wade replied as he walked the officer from the barn and closed the door behind him. "We'll spend the rest of the night here and let our horses rest before heading on in the morning."

Chase nodded. "I'll have a couple of my men bury those two in there."

"Good," Wade answered as they walked around the house. "I'll get the passengers inside and get them settled down for the night."

"Settled down for the night?" Patrick Cliff stood by the stagecoach. "Did I hear you right? We're spending the night here?"

Wade had hoped for a few moments to gather his thoughts before explaining what had happened, but like it or not, the El Paso rancher was pressing for an explanation of the delay. And in the blinking of an eye all the passengers had turned and were staring at Wade.

"I'm afraid that's the way it stands," Wade replied. He outlined their situation, omitting the butchered bodies he had discovered in the barn. "Until our horses are rested, we're stuck here and will have to do the best we can. If everyone would move inside, we'll see what we can do about making you comfortable for the night."

"There's a chance the Comanches will be back, isn't there, Mr. Bonner?" Vera Brown asked.

"I'm afraid so," Wade admitted. "But even if they do, I don't think they'll give us too much trouble. We have Lieutenant Chase and his men with us." He wished he felt as secure about the soldiers' Indian-fighting ability as he sounded.

"The good Lord knows that we've enough weapons and ammunition to supply a whole army." This from Howard Dalrymple, who grinned and tilted his head toward the army wagons.

The concern faded from the older woman's face as the salesman escorted her nephew and her toward the station house, with Harris and Cliff following behind them. However, Laura Parvin hesitated.

There was nothing Wade could say to assure her that they would be safe for the night without resorting to bald-faced lies. "Things are pretty torn up inside. I'll need a hand getting everyone settled in—especially when it comes to rustling up supper. I've never been much when it comes to cooking."

She looked up at him and smiled weakly. "Somehow I get the feeling that you're an excellent cook, Wade Bonner, when the situation requires it. I think getting my mind off those Indians is what you're *really* trying to do."

"I *do* need help," he said, admitting to himself that she had been correct. "You might ask Mrs. Brown to lend a hand. She seemed more worried about the Comanches than anyone else, and it might help to ease her mind a mite if she had something to do."

Laura's smile widened while she studied the man beside her. Eventually she gave her head a little tilt. "All right, I'll go in and talk with Vera. Maybe doing something with our hands will take both our minds off the Indians."

Wade reached out and squeezed her shoulder. "It's going to be all right. Raiding parties usually don't hit the same place twice in one night. The Comanches came here for horses, and they got them."

She reached up, placing her hand on his. Rising to her tiptoes she lifted her face to his and leaned toward him.

"Bonner," Lieutenant Chase called out as he approached, "I've posted two men as guards. They'll be relieved in two hours."

Laura looked at the young officer and then at Wade. With a shrug, she walked into the station. Wade silently cursed Chase's inopportune arrival and the kiss it had cost him.

"Is there anything else you can think of that my men or I should do?" the lieutenant asked.

"You've done all that can be done for the time being," Wade replied. "Now all we can do is wait out the night."

Chapter Ten

Wade shifted his weight from one foot to the other and back again as he used the door frame to get at an irritating itch between his shoulder blades. The nagging spot placated, he stretched as he let his gaze probe the light drizzle that fell from the thinning clouds outside.

Nothing—he saw nothing. Puddles that had been minor lakes mere minutes ago, fed by a sudden deluge from thunderheads rolling in from the north, had already shrunk to mere patches of mud. The ever-thirsty earth sucked away the moisture as rapidly as the storm clouds had released it. By sunrise the only trace of the downpour would be a blue haze over the countryside as the unrelenting sun once more robbed the land of precious moisture.

Wade's eyes lifted. A full moon poked through the clouds above, bathing the world in frosty light. A scene that should have inspired an appreciation of its beauty brought to mind instead the chilling phrase "blood moon." An old dread suffused him. Blood moon was the name Texans gave the full moon—not for its color, but because during the full moon Comanche raiding parties thundered out of the plains, leaving the land painted red with their victims' blood.

It was not the Indians who had struck earlier, slaughtering the man and woman who had run Sheffield Station, that troubled Wade; they had taken the horses they were after and were now probably halfway back to their camp with the prizes they had stolen. But there were numerous Comanche bands in the area, and any one of them might also see the station as an easy target. The night with its full moon could well bring another raiding party after horses that were no longer here. And the night was still young; midnight lay at least two hours away.

Wade turned in the doorway, leaning against the frame as he passed the single-shot rifle he held from his right to left hand. Soldiers and passengers alike lay on the floor of the station, and as near as Wade could tell, all were asleep. It was just as well: Better that minds be occupied with dreams than dwelling on the possibility of death at the hands of Indians.

For a brief instant a fleeting cloud moved across the face of the moon. When it passed, the soft glow once more washed through the open door. A smile touched Wade's lips. Laura and Vera Brown slept across the room with young David nestled protectively between them. In spite of their doubts, the two women had displayed no hint of fear once they had entered the station and taken on the task of seeing to the welfare of the others.

Wade's gaze traced over the delicate features of Laura's face. How beautiful she was. How strange were the sensations she awoke within him—warm and familiar, yet new and unknown. Sarah McGarth had once evoked such feelings, but that seemed a lifetime or two ago.

Love—it was an easy word to utter. But it was a complicated emotion, comprised of many elements. Not the least of these was trust. Love required a man to open himself to a woman completely so that she could see the bad with the good and judge his worth. Until Laura, only Sarah McGarth had ever won such trust from Wade.

And Frank McGarth had made certain that love had no chance to grow. Bitterness filled Wade's mouth. Sarah and he had shared dreams of a life together—dreams that Frank had rent asunder in the space of one black night.

Wade looked back at Laura. Now Frank McGarth loomed before him, ready to destroy the love he felt growing for this gentle woman.

Love? His gaze returned to the night outside. He was deluding himself, for until he reached Fort Davis, he would have no time for the feelings a man shared with a woman. Even if he managed to face McGarth and live, what kind of life could he offer a woman like Laura? He was a wanted man—wanted for murder. Could any woman accept that in a man?

The distinctive clack of hoof on stone swung Wade's head from side to side in search of the sound's source, while a shiver of fear crept along his spine. He saw nothing, but that meant little. The sound had not been imagined. Someone was out there.

Thumbing back the hammer of his rifle, he slipped back into the station. Kneeling at Roy's side, he nudged his friend's shoulder. Roy's eyes blinked open. Wade placed a finger to his lips, signaling Roy to remain silent.

"I think I heard something outside," he whispered. "Take my place at the door. I'm going out to take a look."

Roy lifted the shotgun from the floor beside him and followed Wade to the doorway. "You be careful. Losin' your hair ain't gonna make you any handsomer to that Miss Parvin."

"The same thought occurred to me," Wade replied as he slipped into the night and moved along the front of the building.

Reaching the corner, he paused and glanced down the west side of the station. Nothing. He darted around the corner and moved in a crouch along the wall, in the direction of the barn. He halted again when he reached the rear corner. If Comanches had returned, they would make a try for the horses stabled in the barn.

He cursed under his breath. The mistlike drizzle made it impossible to see whether the latch to the barn doors was still in place. He sucked in a steadying breath and leveled the rifle before him. He had to make certain the horses were all right. With a glance to each side, he pushed from the wall and ran across the open area toward the barn.

"Bonner!" a voice called to him.

Wade stopped and spun around, his boots slipping and sliding in the mud. As he wobbled unsteadily, trying to maintain his footing, he saw the rider—and the rifle aimed directly at his chest.

"Ease the hammer down on the Sharps real gentlelike,"

the mounted man said. "I came to stop trouble, not start it."

"Stop trouble?" Wade did as he suggested. "Pointing the barrel of a rifle at a man is a funny way of stopping trouble."

"Not if a man's just making sure that he doesn't get a bullet in his gut before he gets the chance to speak his piece."

Wade's head cocked to one side. The voice was familiar, and he understood the reason for that when the rider nudged his bay mount forward. The face beneath the rain-dripping hat brim was illuminated by moonlight, and he saw that the rider was one of the passengers he had left far behind in Austin. "Mr. Thacker? What are you doing here?"

It took Thacker a few seconds to answer, and Wade had the feeling that he was weighing something. Finally the man slid his rifle into a saddle holster. "My business can wait until after we solve your problem."

"*My* problem?" Wade was not certain what the man was talking about. "I don't see as how I have a problem."

"That's because you haven't seen what I saw a few miles east of here." Thacker pointed over his shoulder, then dismounted. "There are twenty men out there dressed up like Johnny Rebs just waiting until midnight before they come riding down on you."

"Attack us? Why?" Wade forced confusion into his voice, wanting to see exactly what this man knew.

"It's no time for games, Bonner." Thacker shook his head. "If I had my way, I'd let them get the gold you're carrying, but dammit, man, I've a son and a sister on your stage."

"David?"

"*And* Vera Brown is my sister." Thacker seemed to be trying to contain his impatience, as if giving a lesson to a backward pupil. "Now you can see why I couldn't let those men attack this station."

Wade began to see more—another coincidence that appeared to be less and less of a coincidence. Ugly pieces began to fall into place, all part of a puzzle he had not recognized until this very moment. If he had been a betting man, he would have wagered that there had not been a Comanche near the station tonight. A man and woman had been killed, not for horses but for army gold. Their deaths had carefully been made to appear as though Comanche warriors had killed them. The station's horses had been driven off to strand the stage and gold here for the night. Wade shuddered. What kind of twisted mind worked in such a cold-blooded fashion?

"Twenty men, you say?" Wade's mind raced, desperately searching for a means to escape before the men rode down on the way station.

"Twenty men," Thacker repeated. He pulled a watch from a pocket, opened it, and turned its face to the moonlight. "It's ten-thirty. You have an hour and a half before they attack—more than enough time to hitch up a team and get your passengers out of here."

"*If* I had horses," Wade answered. He gave the man an abbreviated account of all that had occurred at Sheffield Station. "My team wouldn't make it more than four or five miles before they keeled over and died," he concluded. "We aren't going anywhere tonight."

"Son of a bitch!" The loud curse did nothing to relieve Thacker's frustration, for he sat and glowered at Wade.

It was becoming obvious to the driver—as it appeared to be to Thacker—that whoever was behind the planned raid had not thought of it on the spur of the moment; the outlaws must have have schemed long and hard to isolate the stagecoach before striking. Worse, the marauders had already shown they had no respect for human life. They had killed twice just to set up the robbery. Odds were they intended to kill all who were on the stage as well as the soldiers escorting it.

"All right," Thacker finally said. "You load up the stage and wagons and head off the trail and hide for the night."

"Hide? How am I supposed to cover my tracks in this muck?" Wade lifted a boot, to reveal a deep footprint. "Wagon wheels will cut a track inches deep in this."

Thacker pondered this, wiping his hand over his face
with a tired gesture. "You're right," he conceded. "The
ground's too wet."

"I think we should wake the others and get them
ready to fight," Wade suggested. "Maybe the women and
your son could get away and hide themselves. These outlaws won't be looking for them."

Thacker shook his head. "Making a stand here is too
risky. The station and the barn are both wood, and as soon
as those skunks realized we were holed up inside, they'd
burn us out. Then they'd go looking for the women and
the boy—just to eliminate any possible witnesses. They're
born killers. No, if we're going to fight them, we should
pick the time and place."

Wade stared at the man, his meaning slowly becoming clear. "You mean, we attack them?"

"We'll have surprise in our favor. That should whittle
the odds down a mite," Thacker answered with a firm tilt
of his head. "We'll have a chance that way. More than if
we wait here for them to attack and risk them overrunning
us. They set the battle, but we choose the battlefield."

Wade wanted to tell the man he was a lunatic, that
the plan was insane. It was cold, and it was hard. But
upon reflection he realized that it made sense. Kill before
the enemy killed was simple military logic, a logic Wade
could not argue with. He nodded his head in acceptance.

"How many men do you have inside?" Thacker asked.

"Not enough. Under a dozen."

Thacker looked grim. "Well, I suggest we go and
wake them and get them ready to move out."

Again Wade did not argue; there was no time.

Inside the station, while Thacker was reunited with
his son and sister, Wade explained the situation to the
passengers and soldiers. Lieutenant Chase, who needed
no convincing of the soundness of Thacker's attack plan,
ordered his men to ready themselves for the fight. The
men under the young officer's command were obliged to
follow those orders. Such was not the case with the men
who rode the stagecoach.

"I'm asking for volunteers," Wade said. "When it gets

down to it, this isn't your fight. Nobody here will hold it against you, if you decide not to go along."

"Like you said, this ain't my fight," Deke Harris said. "I'll sit this out. Makes more sense just to turn the gold over to them men without gettin' myself kilt first."

When Harris spoke, Wade realized that contrary to what he had just promised, he did resent the man's refusal to join in the fight. But he accepted Harris's decision with a nod of his head and then looked at Howard Dalrymple and Patrick Cliff.

"Count me in." Dalrymple spoke first. "That is if you can talk the army into loaning me one of those rifles out there in the wagons."

"Same goes for me," the rancher said.

"All of you will need horses, too." Thacker said as he gave his son a final hug. "Your teams might not be fit for pulling a load, but they'll do to carry riders for two miles."

Wade noticed that the man did not mention the two miles required to return to the station. If the same thought moved through Thacker's head as did his, it was best to leave unspoken the possibility that none of them would be returning.

"I thought we was done fightin' battles," Roy said to Wade as Chase and his soldiers left the building for the needed rifles and ammunition.

"You are," Wade replied. "I want you to stay here with the women, just in case."

Roy opened his mouth as if to protest, but he closed it again when Wade cut his eyes to Harris. Roy nodded, his lips drawn in a thin, tight line. There was no need for further explanation: Harris had already proven he could not be trusted around women. "I'll stay, but I don't like it," was all that Roy said.

"I'm not asking you to like it," Wade replied, "just do it."

"I'll do it, but that don't make me like it." Roy refused to let his friend have the last word "Don't like it at all."

Wade started to follow Thacker from the way station, when he caught Laura's gaze out of the corner of an eye.

He turned to her. Before he could answer the worried expression on her face, she said, "Please be careful, Wade."

He forced himself to smile. "I intend to do just that."

The glow of the campfire had been visible for the last mile, and Wade, riding just behind Matthew Thacker and Lieutenant Chase, pondered how the marauders had managed to keep the fire burning during the thunderstorm. But then, he was not here to figure out how outlaws kept flames going; he was here to kill them before they killed him.

Both Chase and Thacker raised their arms, signaling the men to halt. The two turned their mounts around to face the men who followed. It was Thacker who spoke:

"We're going to split up here. Lieutenant Chase and his soldiers are going to circle around the camp."

He paused long enough to open his pocket watch and turn it to the moonlight. "We're not going to try anything fancy. In a half hour, I'll open fire. We'll hit them from the west while the lieutenant and his men attack from the east. With luck we'll have them before they know what's happening. Any questions?"

When none came, Thacker looked at the young officer and nodded. "You have half an hour to take your position."

Chase returned the nod and then signaled his command to follow as he reined his mount southward to swing in a wide circle around the camp. Wade watched the soldiers depart until Thacker whispered, "We're going to move in real slow and quietlike until we're a quarter of a mile away."

What he neglected to say was that once they reached that position the wait began. Wade tried to convince himself that fifteen minutes was not a long time. But he knew from innumerable battles that he was wrong. Fifteen minutes or fifteen hours—it made no difference. The waiting and the doubts that gnawed at the mind were always worse than the actual fighting.

Beside him, Thacker sat straight in the saddle, his eyes occasionally dipping to the watch in his right hand.

The one-armed man had seen action in the war—Wade was certain of that, because there was something in his bearing that said he had been through this before. Perhaps he had been an officer Lieutenant Chase had acquiesced to the man's authority without voicing any objection.

To the east Wade saw the occasional form of a man moving in front of the flames. He said a silent thank-you for that fire. The harsh light would blind the twenty marauders to anything beyond its yellow-orange glow, thus concealing the men who surrounded the camp.

"Five minutes more," Thacker whispered. "Check your weapons—quietly."

Wade examined his rifle, found all as it should be, slipped the Colt from his belt, and checked the six rounds in its cylinder. Lastly, he pulled the extra cylinder from his pocket. It, too, held six loads. If they took the men by surprise, the first seven shots would be enough. If not, triple the bullets he carried might not be sufficient to save his life.

A distant voice drifted from the camp, audible over the still prairie: "All right, boys, let's ride. That army gold is just waitin' for us!"

If Wade had held any doubts as to the intent of the twenty men camped here in the middle of nowhere, they were laid to rest with those words. Thacker had not misled him: The men rode for one purpose—to attack Sheffield Station.

The camp abruptly came alive. Men pushed from the ground and hurried toward a remuda of twenty horses.

Thacker snapped his pocket watch closed and shoved it into a coat pocket. "We can't wait any longer. We have to hope Lieutenant Chase is ready. If those men make it to their horses, we won't stand a chance of stopping them. Pick your target and make your shots count."

Reins looped over his left arm, Thacker pulled his rifle from its saddle boot and cocked it. No war cry tore from his lips to sound the charge. He simply slammed his heels into the bay's flanks, and the horse bolted forward.

Wade imitated the man's lead. His legs rose and fell, driving into his mount's sides. Then his thighs and calves clamped tightly about the animal to maintain his seat on the horse's bare back as the beast picked up speed.

They were two hundred yards from the campfire when Thacker shouldered the rifle, pointed rather than aimed the rifle at the man nearest him, and squeezed the trigger. The thunder of exploding black powder rent the night's silence. Three shots in rapid succession answered the report of his rifle as the men who rode at his side emptied their single-shot rifles into the camp.

Not waiting to see if that first shot had struck its target, Thacker thrust the spent rifle back into the saddle holster and freed the pistol on his hip. His ears strained to hear the reports of Lieutenant Chase's rifles. They did not come. He cursed; the marauders, fully visible now in the campfire's flickering flames, turned to face the four men who rode down on them.

Four men against twenty—five to one—the odds were too high for success. Thacker's revolver lifted, and he fired, once, twice, and two of the outlaws dropped.

It was the same determination that guided Wade's gun hand. If he were to die tonight, he would take as many of the would-be highwaymen with him as he could. Blue and yellow flame blazed from the muzzle of the converted Army Colt as he took aim at a man, dressed in the ragged remnants of a Confederate uniform, who was swinging to the back of a chestnut horse. The shot struck true, slamming home between the man's shoulder blades.

Wade's arm swung to the left and his finger squeezed around the trigger again. His second shot went wide, but it was close enough to send a man to the ground to escape a bullet aimed for his head.

The bark of Wade's third shot was lost in a roar of thunder that came from the east. Lieutenant Chase and his men charged. Confused, the marauders spun around, then from one side to the other, unable to decide which attack to face.

It was that very bewilderment that Thacker was counting on, and he took full advantage of it as his gelding bounded into the camp. He fired pointblank into the face of a man who swirled around with an unfired rifle clenched in his hands. He heard the outlaw's scream, but was spared the bloody sight of what remained of the man's face when he reined the bay toward the remuda, to cut off the marauders who were scrambling for their horses.

The idea of fair play never entered Wade's mind as he emptied the pistol's remaining bullets into the chaos that now reigned in the camp. He and the others gave the outlaws the same chance that the outlaws would have given them at Sheffield Station. To his right he saw Howard Dalrymple fire a round into the back of a man's head and, in the next instant, spur his horse over two men who were running for their mounts.

Chase and his men were no more delicate about picking their targets. If a man's chest or back presented itself, they fired. But they were headstrong, and Wade saw at least one private foolishly expose himself in taking aim, only to be cut down. Lieutenant Chase, coming to his aid, also took a bullet.

To one side Wade saw Patrick Cliff take aim and fire and then grip his forearm in pain as another marauder's bullet winged him. But for all that, the attackers were getting the better of their enemy. They kept firing, felling outlaw after outlaw.

Those with finer sensibilities might have labeled their actions a massacre, but to Wade it was a matter of simple survival. The death screams that shattered the night were not his; that was all that mattered. It was a harsh code, but one that would allow him—and his passengers—to live to see another day.

He broke open the Colt, slipped out the spent cylinder and snapped in the spare. To his right two of the band managed to climb into their saddles. He jerked the head of his mount around and fired two rounds. The first caught the closer rider in the neck. The man jerked rigid and in the next instant went limp, crumpling as he slid from his horse and dropped to the ground.

Whether his second shot struck home, Wade never knew. The second rider spurred his mount north, racing beyond the glow of the campfire. Nor did Wade have time to pursue the fleeing man. He was barely able to swing his arm over the neck of his mount and fire into the chest of a bearded man who was rushing him with his rifle raised high, swinging the butt end in bludgeon fashion. The man screamed, dropped the rifle, and fell back, his body twitching spasmodically.

Two more of the outlaws reached their horses. Again Wade's Colt whipped about. He never had the chance to fire. Instead of stepping into the stirrup, the man closest to him abruptly pivoted, leveled a rifle at Wade, and fired.

Wade, reacting rather than thinking, had thrown himself flat against the neck of his horse. Hot lead sizzled above his left ear like an angry hornet. He cursed when he pushed up. The very confusion that had given the attackers an edge over the marauders had almost cost him his life.

Once again lifting the heavy Colt, he took a bead on the second man who had gained his horse's back. Thumbing back the pistol's hammer, Wade's finger tightened around the trigger. Then he froze.

Moonlight or a flaring flame from the campfire—he could not be certain which—washed over the outlaw's face. *Frank McGarth!* Wade's finger jerked down on the trigger, but it was a waste of energy and ammunition. The shot went wild. A heartbeat later, the escaping marauder jerked his horse around and spurred it southward, with his companion riding at his heels.

McGarth? Wade shook his head. It could not have been; the light and his own fixation on what lay ahead had combined to play tricks on him. This camp was east of Fort Stockton, more than a hundred miles away from Fort Davis, where McGarth was headquartered. He had seen Frank McGarth where McGarth could not have been.

Silence.

The lack of gunshots and cries penetrated Wade's thoughts. He looked from side to side; as quickly as it had begun, the fighting had ended.

"We did it." This from Howard Dalrymple, who sounded as though he did not believe his own words. Then, with decidedly more enthusiasm: "By God, we did it!"

Chapter Eleven

Matthew Thacker emptied the spent shells from his revolver and reloaded as he surveyed the bloody scene surrounding him.

It was a complete victory. Twenty living men had been in this camp when he had charged. Fourteen of them now lay dead on the ground; just six of the twenty had escaped, scattering in all directions. The attack had been simple, direct, and effective.

Thacker's eyes lifted to where Wade Bonner sat beside Patrick Cliff, wrapping a bandage around the rancher's right forearm. Tonight's victory had not come without cost, but the bullet Cliff had taken was a small price to pay compared to the toll taken on the soldiers.

Three more men lay on the ground, all wearing blue uniforms—Lieutenant Chase and two privates, whose names Thacker had never even heard, let alone learned. He tried to tell himself that battles—and this had been a battle in spite of the fact that the fighting had lasted less than five minutes—were always like this. That did not ease the weight that pressed down on his shoulders. Nor did he feel any better when he considered that they had had no other choice. Killing, no matter what the reason, never came easy.

"Mr. Thacker"—Wade Bonner rose—"I'd like to get Mr. Cliff here back to the way station. I've managed to stop the bleeding, but his arm needs cleaning and a fresh bandage."

"We'll all ride back to the station," Thacker replied.

"We've done what we came here to do, and the others will be worrying about us."

There was always the possibility that the six outlaws who had escaped might regroup and make a try for the way station, Thacker realized. As slim a chance as he believed it to be, it remained a chance, and David and Vera were still there. He would breathe easier when he was with them again.

"Sir"—a sergeant stepped forward and identified himself as William McCormick—"me and the other men would like to stay here and see that the lieutenant and James and Philips get a proper burial, if that's all right with you."

Thacker would have preferred to have the soldiers back at the station, but their request was a proper one. He nodded.

"What about them?" McCormick glanced at the fourteen dead men in Rebel uniforms. "Want us to bury them, too?"

"Leave them where they fell," Thacker answered, without giving his words a second thought. Standard Ranger procedure was to leave those killed in battle for the coyotes and buzzards. "If their friends want their bodies, they can come back and bury them."

Wade glanced at Thacker, his face showing surprise, and Thacker realized that his decision seemed harsh, even for criminals such as these. The sergeant, however, did not seem to mind. In fact he appeared relieved that he and his companions did not have the responsibility of burying fourteen additional bodies.

When Thacker signaled, Wade helped Cliff to his feet and then boosted him onto one of the saddled horses left by the outlaws. He then climbed astride another of the horses and started to gather the reins of the team animals they had used for the attack. Dalrymple waved him off.

"You worry about getting Pat back," the salesman said. "The soldiers and I'll bring the horses when we come."

"You're staying?" A puzzled expression clouded Wade's face.

Dalrymple nodded and gave a little shrug. "Some-

body needs to stand guard while these men work. It's like
Mr. Thacker said: The others might come back for their
friends' bodies."

Wade smiled sardonically. "I don't think outlaws like
these give a hill of beans for funeral rites—even for their
friends. But do as you see fit." Then he added, "Just be
certain you and those horses are back at the station within
the hour. I'm not that worried about you, but the horses
are needed to get us out of here tomorrow."

Dalrymple smiled. "The horses and *I* will be back."

Thacker waited until Bonner finished talking to the
salesman before easing his bay westward toward the way
station. Neither Bonner nor Cliff spoke on the ride back,
which was just as well. Thacker needed time to plan his
next move.

Sheffield was not the place to reveal himself to the
stage driver—especially not after his fine showing in the
attack. Thacker was not afraid of the young man's ability
with a gun, but he did consider the reaction of the other
passengers. Battle often molded strange bonds of camara-
derie between men. If he should try to arrest Wright so
soon after the fighting, he might find himself staring down
the wrong ends of pistols drawn by Cliff and Dalrymple.
Even the soldiers might defend Bonner, he admitted to
himself. It would be better to wait until the stage pulled
into Fort Stockton and the heat of tonight's battle had
cooled before he made a move.

Thacker stole a glance to his side. Bonner gave no
indication that he had recognized him. As long as that
situation remained unchanged, Thacker held an ace in the
hole. He could wait to play that high card.

An unsteady sensation fluttered in the pit of Wade's
stomach, and it had nothing to do with the fight. Instead,
it stemmed from the sideways looks Matthew Thacker
kept giving him. Something was on the man's mind, and
Wade got the distinct feeling that it involved him.

But what? The answer eluded him. He had never in
his life seen a one-armed man until the war; then he had
encountered a number of them, but he hadn't known

them by name. What possible interest could Thacker have in him?

Wade pursed his lips. Was he just letting his mind play tricks on him again, like thinking he had seen Frank McGarth during the fight? It had to be that, but he could not shake the sensation that Thacker was keeping a careful eye on him.

As the three men neared the way station, Thacker reined in his bay. Even though he was close to home, his horse was tired and needed a rest. And the animal would need all its strength for what Thacker had planned for the days ahead.

Wade came up alongside. "I think it would be wise," he told Thacker, "if I rode up alone and announced us. Otherwise, my friend Roy might decide to welcome us with that shotgun he's carrying."

Thacker doubted that the man intended anything, but just in case he did harbor foolish ideas, he wanted Bonner to know exactly where he would be. He ran his hand over his throat and finally nodded. "Sure, you go on ahead. We'll be right behind you."

Allowing Bonner several yards' lead, Thacker nudged the bay forward again. Fifty yards from the entrance to the way station, Bonner called out to those inside. The man he called Roy stepped out and hailed the stage driver.

"I don't know how, but you did it!" Roy slapped Bonner on the back as Thacker drew the gelding to a halt in front of the station. "To be honest, I wouldn't have laid money on your chances, Wade."

"I wouldn't have either," Wade replied. "But thanks to Mr. Thacker here, most of us managed to pull through."

"Most of you?" This from Deke Harris, who walked outside.

"Three of the soldiers were killed," Thacker answered while he tied the bay to a hitching post. "And Mr. Cliff got hit in the arm."

"Wade!" Laura Parvin ran through the doorway, her arms wide, and Wade turned to her, a grin on his face.

*   *   *

Harris silently cursed as he watched the young woman throw her arms around the driver's neck and plant a loud kiss on his mouth. This was not the way it was supposed to happen. McGarth and the boys were supposed to ride up and take the gold. When they rode away, he was to ride with them.

"Wade, I was so frightened," Laura was saying. "I didn't think that I would ever see—"

Harris turned to the one-armed man again. "What happened?"

"We took them by surprise," Thacker answered. "Six got away and the rest are dead. That's all there was to it. The fighting was over inside of five minutes."

Dead! The word hit Harris like a blow from a sledge-hammer. How could it have happened? Fourteen of the boys dead! Only six had managed to escape. And they had not come for the gold! His head spun. It made no sense; it could not be. Yet these men were alive, and McGarth and the others were nowhere in sight.

"Matthew? Matthew, is that you?"

Out of the corner of his eye, Harris saw Vera Brown standing in the doorway. Behind her stood the boy. Sweat popped out on Harris's forehead while an icy chill flowed through his body. Could he do alone what twenty men had failed to accomplish? Excitement and cold fear battled within him.

"It's me, Vera," Thacker answered his sister. "I'm all right, but I've got a man out here that needs a little patching up."

"Come, David." The woman reached back for the boy's hand. "Your father needs our help."

Harris swallowed. It was now or never. If the gold were to be his, he had to act.

He did. His left arm snaked out, closing around the seven-year-old boy, while his right hand wrenched a .44-.40 caliber pistol from the holster on his hip.

"What is going on—" Vera Brown's eyes went round with fear when she saw Harris press the muzzle of his revolver to her nephew's head.

"Let me worry about what's goin' on here, old woman.

You just get out there with the others," Harris ordered. He turned toward Thacker and Wade, holding the child in front of him as a shield. "Don't none of you do nothin' stupid. Not if you don't want to see me kill this boy."

Thacker's mouth was as dry as cotton. He saw the man's hand trembling as he held the gun to David's temple. One wrong move, and the man could accidentally fire the pistol. "Why don't you just put that—"

"Why don't you just keep your mouth shut and listen up!" Harris held the upper hand, and he knew it. Now he had to make it pay off. "If you—*all* of you—do what I say, won't nobody get hurt. All I want is the gold. Understand?"

Wade edged Laura behind him out of the line of fire in case Harris should decide to turn the gun on them. "Harris, you can't get away with this. There's only one of you and four of us with guns."

"Don't you worry about me gettin' away," Harris sneered. "Just worry about me blowing this boy's head off if you don't do like I want."

"Dammit, Wright, listen to him! Don't do anything stupid. That's my son he's got," Thacker urged.

Wright? Harris saw the stage driver's head snap around. Thacker had called him by another name; maybe Bonner wasn't who he said he was, and Thacker knew it. Whatever the case, it meant nothing to Harris. "You heard the man," he said to the driver. "Don't do nothin' stupid, 'cause I *will* pull this trigger if you force me to." Harris's gaze moved over the faces of the four men opposing him to make certain each of them knew he meant business. "First I want you to throw down your guns."

Harris saw the man identified as Wright step forward. "Look," he said. "Don't be stupid. You do anything to that boy and you'll hang—you know it! If you let him go, just take the gold, maybe if they catch you, you won't swing from a rope. Think about it, Harris!"

Harris glanced around at the others. One man who had slowly been reaching for the revolver in his holster, to get the drop on Harris while his attention was occupied, eased his hand away from his gun.

"To hell with you all," Harris replied. "This boy's my

ticket out of here, you know that as well as I do. So do like I say: Throw down them guns!"

He waited until each man had tugged pistol from holster or belt and tossed it to the ground. "Good, you're startin' to get the idea. Now what I want is them horses in the barn. You two"—he nodded to Wade and Roy—"get 'em. Hitch four to that wagon over yonder. I'm taking it. The other horses get tied to the back. Understand?"

"Understood," Wade answered. He reached out and tapped Roy's shoulder. "Come on."

Harris watched the two disappear behind the way station before looking back at Thacker and Cliff. "You two get the strongbox from the stage and put it in the wagon."

"Can you help?" Thacker looked at Cliff.

The man nodded. "I still have one arm. That makes two between us. We can manage."

Keeping Harris in the corner of his eye, Thacker walked beside the stage and climbed to the driver's seat. The strongbox of gold was the only thing in the front boot. He grabbed one of its handles and strained his back and arm to pull it up and toss it to the ground.

"You ladies," Harris ordered, "I don't like you just standin' around. Get over in the stage and stay there."

As the women complied, Thacker and Cliff half carried and half dragged the strongbox, lifted it, and deposited it atop the crates of rifles and ammunition that filled the wagon bed. Thacker turned back to the gunman.

"Let the boy go, Harris. We'll let you take the gold without any trouble."

A humorless chuckle pushed from Harris's throat. "Damn right you'll let me have the gold, 'cause if you don't, you won't have a son. Now move over by the stage. I don't want you anywhere near the wagon."

"You hurt a hair on that boy's head, and I promise I'll hunt you down if it takes all my life." Thacker did as ordered, his gaze dipping to the guns on the ground. As much as he wanted to try for one, it would be signing David's death certificate.

"Just you forget about your life and start thinkin'

about this boy's life and how short it's gonna be if you don't shut your mouth." Harris pressed the muzzle firmly against David's temple.

Thacker looked at his son. Whether bravery or fear had kept the boy silent through all of this he was not certain. However, he could see tears welling in his son's eyes. Every fiber of Thacker's being screamed for him to act, to snatch David away from Harris. He remained motionless. While Harris's attention centered on him there was no chance of saving the boy. He had to wait for an opening.

The clink and jingle of tack announced Wade's and Roy's return. Each man led two horses in harness, and they proceeded to hitch them to the waiting wagon while Harris kept an eye on them as well as on Thacker and Cliff.

"Now tie them saddle ponies behind the wagon," Harris directed, his pistol remaining at David's temple.

Still Thacker bided his time while the driver and shotgunner gathered the three horses' reins and tied them to the rear of the wagon. His mind raced. If an opening did not come soon, it would be too late.

"Okay, now get over there with the others." Harris motioned Wade and Roy toward the stage, and then said to David, "Now it's up to you, boy. Just do like I say, and I won't hurt you. Understand?"

David bit at his lower lip, his pleading eyes shooting to his father as he nodded.

"Good." Harris grinned. "You and me are gonna take us a little ride in that wagon and maybe take us a look at Mexico." His face showed his elation—justified, Thacker realized, if Harris got away with a robbery that twenty men had failed to pull off.

As Thacker watched the gunman edge David toward the wagon, his heart felt as if it were pounding somewhere in the middle of his throat. Any move he made would have to be made now.

"Get on up there, boy." Harris half turned to lift David onto the driver's board. "If you keep nice and quiet, I might let you drive the team on down the road."

As Harris turned, Thacker dived forward. His right arm stretched full length, his hand closing around the handle of Wade's Army Colt.

"Stupid son of a bitch!" Harris swirled around. The bark of his pistol punctuated his curse.

Thacker groaned, jerked over in the sand, and lay on his back. Blood, black in the moonlight, oozed from his right temple. He lay deadly still.

"Oh, my God! Matthew!" Vera Brown cried from the stagecoach. "He's killed Matthew!"

"That's right, you old biddy, and I'll kill you if you don't stop your wailin'!" Harris trained the gun on the three men who started toward Thacker. "Stay where you are, or you'll get the same."

With his gun trained on the men, he collected the four pistols beside Thacker's unmoving body and threw them into the back of the wagon. "That's just in case any of you are stupid enough to think about following me."

He then backed to the wagon and climbed into the driver's seat with David at his side. Lifting the reins, he popped them on the team's back. The wagon jolted forward, rolling south toward the Mexican border and freedom.

Chapter Twelve

"**W**right . . . Wright," Matthew Thacker mumbled as Wade and Roy carried him into the way station and placed him on top of a table. "Wright . . . Wright . . . Wright."

Vera Brown leaned an ear near her semiconscious brother's trembling lips. "What's he saying? I can't make it out."

"Me neither, ma'am," Wade lied with a shake of his head. The name the one-armed man mumbled was more than clear to him. Each time he uttered that single word, cold chills ran up and down Wade's back. He wondered whether anyone had heard Thacker use the name earlier, just as he was worried that Roy might say something about it now.

Roy's eyebrows arched, but he backed up his friend as he answered Vera Brown's question. "He's out of his head, Mrs. Brown. There ain't nothin' he's gonna say will make sense until he comes around again."

Wade glanced about and took a burning candle from a small table across the room. He held it high and examined Thacker's head wound. "Laura, I need a cloth and some water."

When the young woman brought the items, Wade dampened the cloth and carefully bathed the wound. In spite of an abundance of blood, Harris's shot had not entered Thacker's skull. Instead the bullet had grazed the side of the head an inch above the ear, leaving a bloody three-inch welt.

"That don't look bad enough to even knock him out,"

Roy commented when he leaned down to get a better look at the injury.

"Wright . . . Tom Wright," Thacker continued to mutter.

Wade gently tested the area around the wound with a fingertip, but he found no signs that the bullet had shattered the man's skull. "It doesn't look that bad to me, either. But then, I'm no doctor. You can never tell with head wounds."

". . . It don't seem fair this happening to Matthew now." Wade overheard Mrs. Brown, who was talking with Laura. "Not now, with Matthew come back to find his wife dead after losing his arm in the war. And him being a Texas Ranger for all those years. It ain't fair that he should die now—"

The chills running up and down Wade's spine turned into an ice floe. He lifted the candle higher and studied Thacker's face. . . .

It had been dark that night, and he had been frightened out of his mind as only a nineteen-year-old boy accused of murder could be, but Thacker did resemble the Texas Ranger he had escaped from the night of the shooting. Wade tried to fix in his memory the figure and face of the lawman, but it was hopeless. It had been too long ago, and the Ranger's appearance had not been what had interested him. He had been more concerned with getting as far away from Waco as he could.

". . . And David, what's that awful man going to do to David?" Vera Brown continued. "If Matthew dies, the boy has nobody except me and my husband, Clyde. That's why I was taking David to Fort Stockton, you know. Clyde and I were going to care for the boy until Matthew got back from the war. Now they're both going to die. Sweet Jesus, they're both going to die."

Laura stepped forward, putting her arm around the older woman. "Mrs. Brown, please. Don't upset yourself so—"

"Nobody's going to die!" Wade pivoted to face the women. "Your brother's been wounded, Mrs. Brown, but it isn't serious. There's a doctor in Fort Stockton who'll

look after him. And as for David, I'm going after him."
Wade paused for a breath and to calm himself. His tone
had been too harsh. The woman was afraid, and she did
not deserve the knife edge in his voice. "Mr. Thacker's
head needs bandaging, and I'd like for you to take a look
at Mr. Cliff's arm. Do you think you can do that for me? I
need to see about the other men and the horses."

Mrs. Brown swallowed, wiped away her tears, and
nodded. Wade smiled and motioned for Roy to follow him
outside. The night air seemed warmer than Wade recalled, filled with moisture that pressed down around him.
Or was it the knowledge that Thacker knew his real iden-
tity that tightened his chest and made it hard to breathe?

"You ain't serious about goin' after that boy, are you?"
Roy whispered.

"Somebody has to." Wade scanned the moonlit terrain to the south, unable to find a trace of the wagon
containing Harris and the boy. "Harris isn't the type to let
the boy live after he crosses the Rio Grande."

"Have you gone loco?" Roy stared at his friend. "Did
you hear what that man's been mumblin' in there? He's
sayin' 'Tom Wright.' He knows who you are."

"I know." Wade drew in a deep breath. Something
also told him that Thacker had followed the stagecoach all
the way from Austin for more than just finding his son and
sister.

"Tom"—Roy's tone grew somber—"this ain't no time
to try to be a hero. You need to head south to Mexico, but
not to get that boy. You need to save yourself. I hope you
ain't dumb enough to think bringin' David back is gonna
square you with the law. That's a Texas Ranger lyin' in
there. All he's gonna do is thank you real nicelike while he
snaps handcuffs on you and takes you off to the gallows."

Roy had painted an accurate picture of what Wade
expected. Yet he could not let Harris cross the border, not
with David Thacker. The boy was only seven years old,
and he would certainly be killed if someone did not go
after him.

"I know all—"

Wade's sentence trailed off as his head cocked toward

the east. Horses were approaching. Dalrymple and the soldiers were returning. Denying Roy another opportunity to argue, he walked to the remaining army wagon and lifted a rifle from one of the open crates. From another crate he scooped up a handful of cartridges and stuffed them into a pocket. "Roy, I need a canteen. I saw one in the barn. Get it for me and fill it with water."

Roy shook his head dubiously, but did as Wade asked.

Rifle in hand, Wade greeted the salesman and soldiers. He selected a saddled roan from the outlaws' horses, which the men were leading, and swung into the saddle. Roy returned with the filled canteen as Wade explained all that had occurred while the soldiers had buried their dead.

"Roy, I want you to give the horses three hours' rest, then hitch them up," Wade directed. "If you take it slow and easy, you'll make it to the next way station. Don't wait for me there, but keep on the road to Fort Stockton. Thacker and Cliff both need a doctor. If I get the boy, I'll meet you in Fort Stockton. If I don't—"

He did not finish the sentence. Instead he pulled hard on the roan's reins, turning the horse's head southward.

Before he could dig his heels into the animal's flanks, Laura's voice sounded behind him. "Wade—"

He swung round in the saddle as she stepped to his side, extending her hand to his. "Be careful," she said quietly. "It's not just the boy I'm worried about."

He reached down, took her hand and squeezed it. "Don't worry," was all he could say. He turned again and spurred his horse forward.

Harris had an hour's lead start, but he was driving a tired team that hauled a heavy load. With luck Wade would overtake the gunman before long.

Wade knelt, studying the ground around him. He wiped a hand over his face and cursed aloud in frustration. The thunderstorm that had deluged Sheffield Station had not ranged this far south. The deep-rutted wheel tracks he had been following had vanished. Nor could he find any evidence that the wagon Harris drove had passed this way.

Which doesn't mean he didn't, Wade told himself when he rose and took the canteen from the saddlehorn. With the ground this dry and rocky, the trail was impossible to follow at night, and it would be difficult to spot in daylight.

Wade uncorked the canteen and allowed himself a single swallow of warm water to wash the dust from his mouth and throat. To the west the full moon rode near the horizon, appearing twice as big as it had at the zenith. The eastern sky showed the grays that announced the coming sunrise, still an hour away.

Looping the canteen back around the saddle horn, Wade let his gaze search the land to the south. He saw nothing but flatness sprinkled with scrub brush and cedars. Even the ever-present mesquite trees appeared no more than stunted bushes in this part of Texas. The water-starved vegetation was not enough to conceal a wagon, but the night's last darkness was.

Wait or ride? He could not decide which course to take. To wait for the sun meant allowing Harris to lengthen the distance separating them, but light would at least reveal the faint tracks obscured by the night. By continuing to ride, he would gain ground on Harris—but only if he was on the man's trail.

He tried to imagine what he would be doing if he were in Harris's place. If Harris was smart, he would be varying the route he took southward, turning east and west to trace a zigzag course to the border. This tactic might bewilder anyone who followed. And surely Harris knew that somebody *would* follow. The man had kidnapped a child and stolen a strongbox of army gold—both powerful incentives to search for him.

Knowing that men would be trailing him had to be playing on Harris's mind, Wade realized. Fear was a spur that could not be overlooked, for if Harris were frightened enough, he might recklessly drive his team straight for the Rio Grande, in a desperate attempt to outrun those behind him.

Again Wade cursed aloud. These aimless conjectures were not helping him decide whether to wait or ride.

A whole new possibility, one he had never considered, revealed itself in the growing light to the east: high ground. Less than three miles to the south rose a long, rocky hogback, which had been hidden by the darkness until mere seconds ago. The top of that ridge would provide a vantage point to take in the lay of the land for miles in all directions, and if Wade was as close to Harris as he reckoned, then the wagon should be visible from the hogback.

Wade stepped into the left stirrup and swung astride the roan's back. Clucking the horse forward, he urged the animal to the rise at an easy lope. At the base of the ridge, he slowed the roan to a walk and let the horse pick its way up the limestone-strewn slope.

The ridge was four hundred feet from bottom to top, he estimated, and as his horse climbed, he used each foot of elevation gained to scan the open terrain to the east. But the rising sun revealed only a wasteland of rock, sand, and scrub bushes.

Fifty feet from the crest, Wade halted the roan, dismounted, and tied the reins about a branch of a scrawny, ground-hugging cedar. On foot, rifle in hand, he moved up the hillside in a crouch. A mounted man was an easy target to pick out in this barren country, and he had no desire to allow Harris to see him first.

At the top of the rise, Wade squatted on his haunches and peered westward. He saw the same thing he had seen when he had scanned the east—nothing. Where had Harris gone? How could a man, a wagon, and a boy vanish in this desert, where a lizard was hard-pressed to find a stone large enough to hide beneath?

He rose to his feet and looked all around and down. Then he immediately dropped back to a crouch!

A smile devoid of humor slid across his lips. Harris was even closer than he had believed. He got down on his stomach and crawled to the edge of the crest. Directly below his position, at the base of the hogback, stood the wagon he sought. Harris and David sat in the sand beside it.

Wade's smile widened. The load in the wagon had taken its toll on the four-horse team, requiring Harris to stop and allow the animals to rest. The kidnapper's bad fortune was Wade's good luck. If it continued, he'd have David well on the road to Fort Stockton by noon.

For an instant an image of the manacles and leg irons that in all likelihood Thacker would have waiting upon his arrival at the town flashed in Wade's mind. He closed his eyes to shove aside the vision. He had escaped the Texas Ranger once, and as long as he was armed, he had a chance of doing so again. For seven-year-old David Thacker there was no escape, unless he acted.

Inching forward on his elbows, he nestled the stock of the rifle into the hollow of his right shoulder. His thumb arched up to tug the single-action hammer back to its limit. Sighting along the barrel with his right eye, he took a careful bead on the back of Harris's head. The shot had to be quick, clean, and deadly. Should he miss or merely wound the gunman, David would die; of that he could be certain.

Wade's right forefinger curled around the trigger. He drew a breath and exhaled it to steady himself. No one had ever accused him of being a sharpshooter, and at four hundred feet he had to be—

Wade cursed. He had waited too long. Harris rose. The man grabbed David under the arm and swung the boy into the driver's seat. Before Wade could draw another bead, the outlaw walked around the wagon and climbed up beside the boy.

"Damn!" Wade muttered his frustration under his breath as he let the rifle dip and lowered the hammer.

David was sitting too close to Harris. Wade could not risk a shot.

Scooting backwards, Wade shoved to his knees. The narrow hogback ran half a mile to the southwest, where a narrow pass opened between it and another ridge of similar size.

It was that pass that held Wade's attention—or the

mounds of talus that rose near the base of each ridge. The
piles of eroded rock and sand offered the only conceal-
ment Wade could see for miles around. If Harris kept to
his southward path, he would have to move through that
pass.

Pushing to his feet, Wade remounted the roan and
guided it down the hillside. The moment the horse's hooves
hit flat ground, his heels dug into the animal's side.

While Harris's wagon was still a ways off, trundling
along the western base of the ridge toward the pass, Wade
drove his mount at a full run. Fifty yards from the narrow
opening, he halted and once again tied the roan's reins to
a cedar.

In a running crouch, he darted to the largest mound
of soil and stone. A glimpse down the ridge was all he
needed to assure him that he had reached his goal well
before Harris: The wagon still had a quarter of a mile
before it entered the pass.

Wade climbed halfway to the top of the pile of talus
and squatted behind shattered blocks of white limestone.
He glanced over his shoulder to make certain the roan was
safely out of sight.

His gaze slipped across the pass to the boulders strewn
there. If he had been given a choice, he would have
picked the opposite side for his ambush, since it would
have placed him on Harris's side of the wagon. But he had
not had the time.

The clink and jingle of the team's harnesses alerted
him to the closeness of the wagon. Wade placed his rifle
on the ground at his feet. While David remained between
him and Harris, he could not chance a shot. Even in
cartridge form, black powder was less than reliable, and a
misfired round could cost the boy his life.

The hollow clomp of hooves on the dry sand drew
closer. Wade tensed, the muscles in his calves and thighs
taut like coiled springs. His temples pounded and sweat
glistened above his upper lip.

The first pair of horses came into view, followed
closely by the second. Two heartbeats later, the driver's
seat was visible. Harris and David stared ahead.

Now or never! Wade's brain screamed as he leapt to his feet. With two quick strides, he launched himself into the air, sailing across the three feet separating the talus from the wagon. His open arms locked around Harris as he hit the back of the wagon.

Wade's plan of dragging the robber from the driver's board into the back of the wagon had not taken momentum into account. But it came into play as the force of his assault carried him and the man he clutched in a bear hug over the side of the road wagon, spilling them to the ground.

Left shoulder first, Wade slammed into the sand. He groaned, his arms slipping from around Harris's chest. He felt the man roll away from him. Gritting his teeth against the paralyzing pain in his left arm, he rolled to his knees and scrambled to his feet.

"I warned you, little man." Harris knelt in the sand, hate-filled eyes glaring at Wade. "Now you're gonna pay for bein' so stupid!"

The man's right hand dropped to the pistol holstered on his hip. Reacting quickly, Wade took a stride forward with his left leg and lashed out with his right foot. The rounded toe of his boot connected solidly with Harris's hand just as the nickel-plated muzzle cleared leather.

Harris yowled in surprised pain. His arm jerked high, sending the revolver flying through the air beyond his or Wade's grasp.

As he had on that porch in Austin, Wade underestimated the man's ability to recover from an assault that would have immobilized another man. The howl had not died on Harris's lips when his left arm swept out, and his balled fist hammered into the vulnerable flesh behind Wade's left knee.

With one leg still in the air, Wade was unable to maintain his balance. His left leg buckled under him, and he tumbled, crying aloud as his left shoulder again bore the brunt of his fall. Once more he fought through the white-hot pain that lanced down his left arm and rolled away from his opponent.

The hiss of steel escaping leather attracted Wade's

gaze like lodestone drawing iron. Harris now stood; sunlight glinted off the long blade of a hunting knife clutched in his right hand. Harris uttered no threats or warning when he attacked this time, but simply charged at Wade, knife point aimed directly at his neck for a quick kill.

Wade twisted, and tucking his knees to his chest, he kicked out hard with both feet. The soles and heels of his boots slammed into Harris's chest. Instead of driving home that sliver of tempered steel, the man fell back, fighting to keep his legs under him.

Not waiting to see if Harris fell, Wade rolled to his side and shoved to his feet. His right hand found and freed the hunting knife from the sheath that dangled from his belt.

Like a madman, Harris renewed his attack. He flashed his knife blade back and forth as he advanced. Wade backstepped, bobbing to the left and right to avoid the dancing blade. First Harris lashed high, aiming the knife at Wade's face. Then, without hesitation, his arm whipped back in a low, underhanded blow meant to open Wade's stomach.

Conscious or unconscious of his action, Harris set a rhythm to his assault, one that Wade could let his own body match while he bided his time, waiting as he dodged slash after deadly slash. Time took its toll. Like a clumsy boxer throwing his full strength into blows meant to take out a quicker opponent, Harris squandered his energy and, rapidly tiring, slowed down.

This was what Wade was waiting for. As Harris's arm swung back for another high-low combination of blows, Wade abruptly stopped his retreat. He ducked beneath the slash meant for his face, then lunged forward. His own blade plunged into Harris's armpit and sliced deeply into the soft flesh.

"Bastard!" Harris shouted as he clutched at the wound.

Bewilderment clouded his face as he stared at the bright red blood that covered his left hand when he pulled it away. His eyes lowered as he lifted his right arm. Crimson soaked both the arm and side of his shirt. He looked up and stared at Wade as though totally baffled by the wound and the inordinate amount of blood that flowed from it.

There was nothing baffling to Wade. In that one quick slash, he had opened both vein and artery, and not even the most skilled surgeon could have closed that wound in time to save the man. Harris was bleeding to death.

Harris's head moved from side to side as though to deny the inevitable. He took a step toward Wade and then another. His body swayed as he looked down again at the crimson flow that now drenched his side. Blood ran down his arm and dripped from his fingertips. His head lifted. In the next instant, his eyes rolled back in his head, and he fell face down in the sand—dead.

Wiping the knife blade clean on a pantleg, Wade returned it to its sheath. As Thacker had done earlier with fourteen other outlaws, Wade turned and left Harris where he had fallen. A frightened boy waited for him in the wagon, and it was a long way to Fort Stockton.

Chapter Thirteen

"**D**avid! David!" Vera Brown and her husband, Clyde, ran across the enclosure at Fort Stockton and swept the boy protectively into their arms "Oh, David, you're all right!"

The top brass at the post was more interested in the rifles, ammunition, and gold for which it had been waiting. The commander and his aide, both in spotless blue uniforms with shiny brass buttons, came forward to examine the wagon and then quickly ordered a sergeant to see to the unloading.

What was not waiting at Fort Stockton were the manacles and leg irons Wade had been expecting. Although he scanned the faces of the men and soldiers who rushed forward to shake his hand and slap his back, he did not see Thacker in the crowd.

"I don't know how you done it, but you done it!" Roy grinned widely as the crowd that greeted Wade's triumphant return dispersed. That grin faded when he noticed his friend's gaze searching the adobe-walled army fort. "The Ranger ain't come around, Wade."

"What?" A questioning eyebrow rose above Wade's right eye.

"The company surgeon can't make head or tails out of it." Roy shook his head. "He says he can't find a thing wrong with Thacker, that the man should be up and walkin' around. Only Thacker ain't. He's still out cold, stretched out on a bed over in the infirmary."

Roy paused, tilted his head toward the fort's hospital, and looked back at Wade. "Which means we should be gettin' the hell out of—"

145

Wade did not listen. Laura was there, waiting by the stagecoach. Tears of joy glistened in her eyes as she opened her arms, and the invitation was one that Wade could not ignore. He went to her, his own arms closing around her slender waist and drawing her close to him. They kissed long and deep. When they parted, it was only for a brief second, then their mouths pressed tightly together once again.

"I didn't think . . . you'd come . . . back," she sobbed between a barrage of kisses with which Wade outlined the shape of her lips. "I don't know what I would have done, if you hadn't. Wade, I was so frightened."

He held her wrapped in his arms, her head nestled against his chest. His fingertips read the trembling that quaked through her diminutive body. "It's all right. It's over now."

"I know, I know." She nodded. "But if something had happened to you, I—"

Her words faded to an inaudible whisper as another frightened tremble shook her body. When it passed, her head lifted, and her emerald eyes gazed up at Wade. "I don't know how or when it happened, but you've become terribly important to me, Wade Bonner." She paused to draw a heavy breath. "Wade, I love you—"

Wade stiffened. His reaction was involuntary. Why the very words he wanted to hear from this beautiful young woman sent a chill through him, he did not know.

"I know that a lady shouldn't tell a man . . ." Once again Laura's words trailed off. She stared at Wade's face, a perplexed expression shadowing her own. Her arms slipped from around him and she backed away. "What's wrong?"

"Nothing," he said tersely—but there was.

It was more than apparent she sensed the lie in that single word. Hurt replaced the confusion on her face. "Wade, I didn't mean to . . . I thought . . . I mean . . ." she stumbled, searching for the right words. "I thought you felt the same."

He did, and that was the source of the icy chill in his breast. That same iciness gave his voice the sharp edge of tempered steel. "I do feel the same. But there's no place for those feelings in my life right now."

"No place in your life?" Laura's head moved from side to side in denial of his pronouncement.

"There's something I have to do," he tried to explain, but could not without telling her that he was a hunted man. "When we get to Fort Davis—there's something I have to do, Laura. Something you wouldn't understand."

"Tell me," she pleaded. "Let me try to understand. I deserve that, don't I?"

She deserved that and more from him, but that was the one thing he could not tell her. Nor did he know how to extract himself gracefully from the corner he found himself in. "Laura, please trust me. When we get to Fort Davis, you'll understand. Hurting you is the last thing in the world I want to do, but I can't explain—not yet."

"Why?" Tears returned to her eyes; Wade read no joy in them. "You ask me to trust you, but at the same time, you're telling me that you can't—"

"Mr. Bonner?" A man's voice hailed Wade.

Gratefully he turned from Laura. An army captain stood behind him. "Yes."

"A fresh team will be waiting for the stagecoach whenever you're ready," the officer said. "There's also an escort ready to accompany you into Fort Davis."

"Escort?" Wade had seen enough army escorts and their road wagons.

The captain pointed to four soldiers near the stable, saddling their horses. "There has been a lot of Comanche activity between here and El Paso for the past two months. We have orders to escort all civilians to Fort Davis. From there, another escort will accompany you into El Paso."

Without glancing back at Laura, Wade started past the captain. "All right, we'll be ready." He looked up at the sun. "It's near noon. Any chance my passengers and I can eat before we go?"

"The mess sergeant is serving lunch now, sir."

"Thank you. If your men can see to the team while we're eating, we'll be able to leave as soon as we're done.

I'll ask Roy to see to the loading. We'll need to hurry; we have a lot of time to make up."

He did not mention that the farther Matthew Thacker was behind him, the better he would feel.

Roy sat silently at Wade's side while the gray dusk was swallowed by a moonlit night. He had been unusually quiet since the stage had pulled out of Fort Stockton shortly after midday. Wade had no complaints. His mind wandered ahead of the stagecoach, Laura and the two other passengers inside the coach, and the four mounted soldiers that trailed behind. His thoughts centered on Fort Davis and what he would find when he arrived there.

"How far you reckon it is to Casort Station?" Roy asked.

"Ten miles—two hours ahead at most," Wade answered.

"And Fort Davis?"

"Should be there by midafternoon tomorrow."

"Then we should both get as much sleep as we can when we reach the way station."

When they arrived at Casort Station, Wade saw that it was hardly the way station he was expecting. It was in fact a ranch run by a husband and wife along with their five children. Most of the other way stations in this sparsely inhabited portion of west Texas were also ranches, their owners earning extra money by opening their homes to stagecoaches. The stage and its passengers would spend the night at the Casort ranch.

The passengers, Roy, and Wade were served an excellent evening meal, after which the passengers retired to their rooms. The night was hot and still, and although all the windows in the ranch house were open, the sleeping rooms cooled off slowly. Finding his own room uncomfortably stuffy, Wade went out into the yard for some cool air, as the desert quickly gave up its heat to the clear night sky.

Presently Roy joined his friend. "Have you figured out what we're going to do when we get to Fort Davis?" he asked.

"Well, I guess *I'll* find Sims and talk with him first."

Wade emphasized the "I" slightly to make certain that
Roy knew that what waited in Fort Davis did not involve
him. "After that I'll see what happens."

"We'll both talk with Sims; then *we'll* see what happens" was Roy's firm reply.

Wade had no doubt Roy considered himself part of
whatever was going to happen, and he did not argue. Nor
would he hold it against his companion if later on Roy
decided to change his mind.

"What happened the night Ben Alexander was killed,
Wade?"

Wade glanced at his friend. The question had come
out of nowhere, bringing a deluge of memories—some
vividly clear, as though the events had occurred but moments ago, others blurred by time. He knew that sooner
or later Roy would ask about the shooting of the McGarth
plantation foreman; he was just grateful that Roy did not
ask why he had killed the man.

"I had been out to the McGarth place to visit with
Sarah," Wade began. "On my way back home, I stopped
in Waco for a beer."

Both Frank McGarth and Ben Alexander had already
come into the saloon, Wade explained, and they acknowl-
edged his presence with a nod. "They seemed more interested in their own beers than me—until I walked outside."

As Wade had started to mount his horse, Frank had
pinned his arms from behind. Wade could still hear the
hate that hissed in Frank's voice and smell the stale beer
on his breath as he snarled, "I don't want any white trash
around my sister, and I'm going to make sure you understand that."

Frank had swung Wade around so that he faced Alexander. A pleased grin spread over the foreman's face like
oil on water. He balled his fists, slamming the right and
then the left into Wade's stomach. Again and again the
blows pounded into his gut.

"I'm not certain when Frank let me go," Wade said,
shaking his head. "I just remember doubling over and
falling to the ground. My insides felt like they'd been torn
to shreds."

Over his own moans Wade had heard the thunder of a pistol. He looked up to see the surprised expression on Alexander's face as he clutched his chest, blood oozing through his fingers as he toppled to the ground.

"Frank tossed a gun down beside me," Wade continued. "I can still remember his exact words: 'Try to explain your way out of this, lowlife!' The gun was mine. I don't know when Frank took it out of my holster. I pushed to my knees, scooped up the pistol, and swung it around— Frank was gone!"

Before Wade had had a chance to decide what to do, the batwing doors of the saloon had swung open, and the bartender and five men rushed outside.

"At that moment, I just panicked. Alexander was dead and I was holding a still-smoking gun. I knew what it looked like to those men. The next thing I knew I was covering them, threatening to kill them if they moved. I climbed onto my horse and rode northward out of town."

Roy scuffed at the sand with his feet. "And you kept on riding right out of Texas?" he asked,

Wade shook his head. "That's not quite the way it happened. About three miles out of town, I realized that it wasn't me that should be running. I hadn't done anything. I pulled up and was trying to decide just what to say when I rode back into town. I didn't get the chance to decide."

A Texas Ranger had ridden up behind Wade. Wade was ordered from his horse. When he complied, the Ranger stepped from the saddle, boasting how fortunate it was that he had been in Waco when the shooting occurred.

"He was about to snap handcuffs around my wrists when I grabbed his gun. Instead of his taking me back, I left him handcuffed around a sapling. It was then I fled. I realized that there was no way anyone in Waco would believe me, not against the word of Frank McGarth." Wade looked at Roy and shrugged. "Even looking back at it now, I don't see what else I could have done, except run."

Roy nodded. "What about Thacker?"

Wade shrugged again. "I'm not sure. I think he might

be the Ranger I left hugging that tree. I don't know. It was dark, and I don't remember his face that well."

"Then it's just as well we left him back there in Fort Stockton. He'd only complicate things when we go after Frank McGarth."

Matthew Thacker awoke with a start, and he spoke aloud his first thought: "Tom Wright!" His eyes went wide open, darting from side to side. He sat straight up in the cot he lay on and looked around frantically. He did not recognize where he was, but then he remembered—Harris and David. He had leapt for a gun and then—

He brought his fingers to the side of his head and found the bandage. He could not remember anything about how it got there.

"Mr. Thacker!" A man in a white smock carrying an oil lamp rushed across the dim room toward him. "Please lie back down. You've been unconscious for nearly twenty-four hours, and you mustn't move until I've had the opportunity to examine you."

"Examine?" Thacker blinked. "You're a doctor?"

"Captain Thaddeus Quincy."

The man tried to ease him back down on the cot, but Thacker brushed away his arms. "My son, David—I must go after my son."

"There's no need, Mr. Thacker. Your son is right here in Fort Stockton. He's safe and sound with his aunt and uncle," the physician said. "Please lie down and let me take a look at you."

Thacker ignored the man's request. "David's safe? How?"

"That stagecoach driver—I forget his name—brought him back when he brought in the gold. The boy was unharmed."

"Tom Wright brought him here to Fort Stockton?" Thacker was not certain whether to believe what he heard. There was only one way to find out. He swung his legs to the floor. He brushed the doctor away again when the man tried to stop him from standing. "Where do my sister and her husband live? I want to see David."

"Mr. Thacker, you don't understand the seriousness of your condition," the doctor insisted. "You have suffered a head injury. I need—"

Thacker's hat, coat, and gun belt were on a wooden trunk at the foot of the cot. He scooped them up and walked toward the open door.

"Mr. Thacker, please, you're taking a grave risk. You may do yourself serious harm." The doctor's expression was ominous.

Thacker ripped the bandage from his head and tossed it to the floor as he walked outside into the night. First he would find Vera and see if what the physician said was right. If David was here in Fort Stockton, then his next job was to find Tom Wright.

Chapter Fourteen

"**T**hree days' layover?" Patrick Cliff sputtered at the army captain. "What in the blazes for, man?" He was standing next to the stagecoach with the two other passengers, Roy, and Wade. The coach had just arrived at Fort Davis, and the tired passengers were disembarking.

"Comanches, sir," Captain Able Oliver, commander at the fort, answered in a crisp, calm voice of authority. "Raiding parties coming out of the northern plains have been so numerous that we have orders not to allow this stagecoach to leave Fort Davis without a full mounted escort. We won't be able to provide that until the men who are presently out on patrol have returned and are rested. That will take three days, sir."

Cliff mumbled a string of curses.

Captain Oliver ignored them. "Accommodations have been arranged for everyone here within the fort," he said courteously. "If you'll follow me, I will show you to your quarters."

Three days. Wade rolled the delay over in his mind. It should be more than enough time to do what he had come for. "Captain Oliver, Roy and I are going to have to take the stage on into town. We must see to the team."

The blue-uniformed officer faced the two men. "Quarters have also been arranged for you."

"We'll probably take you up on that later," Roy answered. "I think what Wade was tryin' to say is that we'd both like to take a look at the town. It's been a mighty long and *dry* trail 'tween Waco and here."

Oliver smiled when Roy placed triple weight on the

word "dry." Rubbing a hand over his throat, he replied, "I think you gentlemen will find liquid refreshment at the Casa de León. It's the only cantina in town."

Wade nodded with satisfaction. The cantina was where he would find his younger brother Sims, if what Will Boyd had said was true. And there was no reason to doubt the man's word.

Captain Oliver turned to the other passengers. "Madam, gentlemen, if you'll kindly follow me."

Both Howard Dalrymple and the rancher did as the captain suggested, but Laura stood her ground. She glared at Wade, who in turn nervously shifted his weight from one foot to the other. No more than a dozen terse words had passed between them since he had brought the gold and David Thacker into Fort Stockton.

"It's not 'liquid refreshment' you're after in town," she said as she stepped to Wade and Roy. "It's a man named Frank McGarth. Isn't it, *Tom Wright*?"

Wade reeled. Laura pinned him with her gaze to make doubly certain that he knew she spoke to him. How did she know?

"I heard you two talking last night," she answered his unspoken question. "I don't know about Mr. Dalrymple and Mr. Cliff, but I couldn't sleep in the heat back at the ranch, and I heard every word you told Roy, Tom Wright."

"Then you know why I have to go into town." He did not know what else to say to her.

"No, I don't. I don't know anything of the sort." The anger in her tone was undiminished. "How will killing Frank McGarth change anything? You'll still be wanted for murder as Tom Wright; and after McGarth is dead, Wade Bonner will be known as a killer, too."

He had considered these facts. If he killed McGarth, there would be no escape for him in Texas or New Mexico Territory, as he had originally planned. But now it no longer mattered to him. Frank McGarth's outstanding debts to the Wright family were too long overdue, and Wade just had to collect on them.

"There are laws to handle men like Frank McGarth," Laura continued. "Let the law deal with him, Wade.

Don't destroy your life for a man like Frank McGarth. He isn't worth it. A hundred Frank McGarths aren't worth one Wade Bonner or Tom Wright."

"Laura—" he began.

She did not give him the opportunity to continue. "Wade, you can't throw your life away. Think of Santa Fe and the land you'll find there—what *we'll* find there. I love you, Wade—don't you understand that? What happened in the past doesn't matter to me. We can make a life for ourselves in Santa Fe—I know we can. I know it!"

Her words tore at him, for she was saying the one thing in the world that he yearned to hear. She did not care about what had happened five years ago; all that mattered was here and now.

But that was exactly what wrenched his insides. Here and now was Fort Davis; here and now was Frank McGarth, a man who had branded him a murderer, killed his father and brother, and left another brother a cripple. No man could could turn his back on such things and still call himself a man.

"Laura"—Wade gently took her shoulders—"I want you to know that I love you, and that a life with you is more than I ever hoped for. But it can't be—not until Frank McGarth pays in full for what he's done. You have to understand that. I have to find McGarth, there's nothing else I can do."

Laura pushed his hands from her and edged away, shaking her head and trembling as tears welled in her eyes. "No, no, that's *not* the way it has to be at all. You have a choice, Wade Bonner, but you simply refuse to see it. The past means more to you than the present and the future. Death means more to you than life!"

"Laura, please." He reached for her again, but she stepped back from him. He took a step forward. "I have to find McGarth. Don't you see the law would never believe a wanted murderer over the word of a man like McGarth? I have to do it my way."

She stiffened. Now there was no hint of trembling in her voice, just the hard edge of ice. "Then do what you want. I don't care. You're not the man I thought you were. Go on, Wade, go into town. Get yourself killed, if that's what you want."

She did not let him answer. Instead she pivoted sharply and ran after Captain Oliver and the other passengers. The sounds of her sobs hung in the air behind her.

Wade stared after her. He suddenly wanted to shout, to tell her that he'd forget about McGarth, that Laura and he would flee to New Mexico and find a life for themselves. But he neither moved nor spoke. He had made his choice. He turned to the stagecoach and climbed to the driver's box. "Our business is in town."

Roy glanced at his friend, but said nothing as he took his place on the box and lifted his shotgun.

Wade needed no other answer. Roy had also made his choice—whether out of friendship or for some private reason, Wade did not know, nor did he ask. Roy would stand with him, and that was enough.

Lifting the reins, Wade popped the leather against the backs of the team. Six horses strained against their harnesses, drawing the stagecoach forward before swinging to the fort's gate and rolling outside.

As the coach rattled toward town, Wade's gaze took in the rugged granite peaks that were the Davis Mountains —peaks named after Jefferson Davis, as was the fort, in the days when he was United States secretary of war, prior to his years as president of the Confederacy. The mountains rose abruptly from the flat, arid plains, with no foothills to soften the transition from the flatlands. There was no gradual sloping to warn a man of the barrier nature had placed before him; the mountains were just there, abrupt and massive.

Water was as precious as gold in this land. Both the town and the fort drank from a mother lode called Limpia Creek—*limpia*, the Spanish word for "clean." The serpentine path the stream took through the mountains was easily discernible by the giant cottonwoods and elms that grew along the Limpia's rock-strewn banks.

McGarth needs water, Wade thought, trying to imagine just where the man he hunted and his band of men

would make their headquarters. He did not look forward
to scouring unfamiliar territory in search of his enemy, but
if that was what was required, then that was what he
would do.

The coach was rapidly approaching the cluster of adobe
and rock buildings that formed the town of Fort Davis.
Roy tilted his head toward a building at the end of the
main street. "The cantina," he said.

As the coach rattled onto the main street, they could
see a whitewashed sign on the cantina with the words
Casa de León written in bright red letters. Wade drove
the horses on by, continuing past the saloon next door to
the center of town, where the stagecoach office stood.

The town was far smaller than Wade had expected,
no more than a stone jail and courthouse with a few stores
and homes built at the junction of three roads that ran
east, west, and south. Which of the roads led to McGarth?

Wade drew the team to a halt in front of the stage
office, ignoring the man who stepped from inside and
directed him to drive the stage to the livery stable. Instead Wade jumped to the ground and walked down the
sandy street to the cantina he had passed moments ago.
Roy followed at his side.

As they entered the saloon, a heavyset man with a
mustache that drooped below the corners of his mouth
greeted them. "Can I help you, señores?" he asked. "Tequila, mescal, beer?"

"Sims Wright." Wade's eyes adjusted to the cantina's
dim interior. No patrons sat at the Casa de León's five
tables.

"Señor?" The proprietor cast a puzzled expression
across the boards balanced on two barrels that served as a
bar.

"Sims Wright," Wade repeated. "I'm looking for a
man named Sims Wright. I'm his brother."

"Sims's *hermano*?" The bartender's expression grew
more bewildered. "But Señor Hap is dead."

"My name's Tom Wright," Wade answered. "I want
to talk with my brother Sims."

The man hesitated, as though uncertain whether to

believe Wade or not. Finally he lifted an arm and pointed to a door at the rear of the cantina. "He usually sleeps outside, near my kitchen, señor."

Wade crossed the floor of the cantina and opened the door.

The yard behind the cantina was littered and filthy. Wade saw a man lying curled in the shade of an adobe hut with a smoking chimney poking from its roof. The man's snores were audible above the buzz of flies that swarmed around a pile of garbage nearby.

Walking over to the him, Wade stared at the inert figure. In spite of the greasy rags covering the man's body and the dirt caked on his face and hands, Wade had no doubt that this was Sims—or what had become of him.

Wade's nose wrinkled in disgust when he knelt beside his brother. His face was heavily bearded, his clothes greasy and torn, and the odor surrounding him equaled the stink that rose from the garbage heap.

Roy, who had followed Wade out of the cantina, stood over the two brothers. "He don't look to be in much shape, Wade. Worse than Will Boyd said."

Reaching out a hand, Wade nudged Sims's shoulder three times before his brother's eyes opened to slits. "Sims, it's Tom. Get up from there. We need to talk."

"Huh?" Sims's eyes opened, and he blinked. He squinted up at Wade, frowning and bewildered; then a smile edged the confusion from his face. "Tom? Is that really you?"

"It's me. Come on, get up. This is no fit place for a man." Wade pulled on Sims's arm, bringing him to a sitting position. "Come on. We'll go inside where it's cool."

Pushing away Tom's helping hand, Sims stumbled to his feet on his own and then stood for a moment, swaying unsteadily. Wade felt something tear inside his gut. This was not the young, blond-headed boy he had left at home when he had fled Waco. This was an old man with hollow eyes and sunken cheeks.

Like a twisted, winter-withered limb, Sims's left arm dangled uselessly from his shoulder. His right leg appeared to be in little better shape: While the leg supported his weight, both the thigh and calf were no longer straight, but were bent at unnatural angles.

Sims took a step, limping heavily on his bad leg. "Guess I haven't mended too well, have I, Tom?" He glanced down at his leg and arm as though embarrassed by his brother's unexpected arrival. "I must look like hell."

"You'll do," Wade answered, taking Sims's right arm and leading him to the cantina's back door. "You'll feel a lot better once you get some food in your belly. When was the last time you ate, anyway?"

"I'd rather have something to drink," Sims said.

Wade called to the proprietor, who was now serving two customers near the front door. "We could use some coffee over here when you get a minute," Wade said, "and some food." He guided his brother to a table and sat him in a chair against the wall. Roy and Wade took seats facing him.

"I don't know about the food," Sims said. "I was thinking more along the lines of tequila, or mescal."

"Coffee," Wade repeated when the cantina's owner approached their table. "And whatever food you have handy—for all three of us "

"Maybe a beer?" Sims asked meekly. "A beer won't do any harm."

"Later," Wade said with a shake of his head. "I've come a long way to talk with you, Sims. I'd rather you were sober."

Sims bit at his lower lip. "I reckon I can guess what you want to talk about. It's about Hap, isn't it?"

"Yes, and about Pa and our farm," Wade replied. "Will Boyd back in San Antonio told us what he knew. I just want to make certain from you."

A dry, humorless chuckle rasped from Sims's throat as he stared at the scarred tabletop. "If you talked with Will, then you know the whole of it. He was here in Fort Davis when it happened—him and the other boys from Waco. But they all had the good sense to get the hell out when they saw what happened to Hap. As for me, well—"

Sims fell silent when the cantina owner returned to

the table with three plates of pinto beans, barbecued brisket, and tortillas that he placed before the three. He also brought three earthen cups and a pot of coffee, which he set at the center of the table.

"And you?" Wade prompted, when the proprietor had gone. "Why did *you* stay here, Sims?"

"Frank McGarth," Sims said, poking a fork at his meal. "I wanted Frank McGarth—to pay him back for all he done."

Sims paused to wash a bit of beef down with a swig of coffee. "Only I wasn't strong enough to take him, Tom. God help me, but I couldn't do it. At first I hurt too much; then the hooch got hold of me. I drank it to stop the pain, and then I couldn't stop. I even have Frank McGarth to thank for that. He was the one who paid for the booze at first, laughing behind my back. Soon he was laughing at my face at what I'd become."

Wade tried not to pity his brother, but he could not help himself. Will Boyd had been right. Sims had been transformed into something less than a man—all at the hand of Frank McGarth.

"Tom, you don't know how many times I've planned and schemed to kill that son of a bitch." Sims's voice quavered, and his hands shook. "But I couldn't. I couldn't! Not even for what he did to Hap."

Sims's head slumped to his chest, and he began to sob.

Wade reached out and squeezed his brother's shoulder, wanting to say something to reassure him, but unable to find the words.

It was Roy who spoke. "That's in the past, Sims. There's three of us here now for Frank McGarth to reckon with. That's why your brother and me drove a stagecoach all the way from Waco."

Sims's head lifted, an uncertain smile hanging at the corners of his mouth. His rheumy, bloodshot eyes seemed to clear slightly, becoming more animated as he nodded. "Yeah, there's three of us now."

"Or there will be, once we get you cleaned up,"

Wade added. He pointed to Sims's plate. "Eat up. You're going to need your strength."

Sims wolfed down a forkful of beans. "I'll need a gun. I had to sell mine."

Wade did not ask why his brother had sold his pistol. It was obvious what Sims had used the money for.

Roy leaned his shotgun against the table beside Sims. "You got a gun now."

Sims's trembling fingers brushed the scattergun's two barrels. "That'll do. A man ain't likely to miss with this."

"Your food." Wade directed his brother's attention back to the meal before him as he poured another cup of coffee. It would take more than food and coffee to return Sims to his former self, but Wade had to begin somewhere. "Is McGarth here in town?"

Sims shook his head as he worked at the brisket. "He has a little spread about ten miles south of town. It isn't much, just enough to run stock while he gets ready to move them north. Only there isn't much stock now that the war's over. No call for cattle or horses without the Confederate Army to buy them."

Pausing, Sims looked at his brother. "The word is McGarth's thinking about finding another line of work. From what I heard, he's after a shipment of army gold. But I'm not sure about that. It's just something I overheard a couple of his men whispering about in here one night."

Roy glanced across the table at his friend. Wade silently cursed. His eyes had not been playing tricks on him at Sheffield Station. He *had* seen McGarth that night! And he had let the man escape!

"You heard right, Sims," Wade told his brother. "McGarth's men killed a stationmaster and his wife, back at Sheffield, just to set up an attempt on the gold we were carrying. We went after them—a couple of the passengers from our stage, the soldiers acting as escort, and Roy and I. We caught them unawares, and McGarth was with them. I didn't believe it at first." Wade went on to give an account of Harris's kidnapping of the boy and the theft of the gold, as well as his flight toward Mexico, Wade's pursuit, and Harris's death.

"It won't be easy going after a man like McGarth," Sims said, when Wade had finished. "He has about thirty men working for him." He looked at his brother again. "And they aren't good men, Tom. Any one of them would kill his own mother if there was a dollar to be made."

Minus the fourteen men left two miles east of Sheffield Station, Wade thought. That left about sixteen men—seventeen including McGarth. And that was only if all of those who had escaped the attack on the camp had returned to Fort Davis.

Even if only half the six who had escaped that night were still with McGarth, the outlaw leader still had over a dozen men. The odds were impossible to ignore. There were only three to oppose them—two, really, Wade realized, because in spite of the shotgun he now had, Sims could never stand up for long in a fight. Maybe in a month or two, when he had dried out, but not now.

Two men against a dozen . . . Wade would have to make do with that.

"We'll go in at night," he finally said. "We'll get McGarth while his men sleep."

Roy did not appear as certain as Wade sounded when he turned to Sims. "We'll need to know the layout of Frank's spread."

A clink of a coin tossed on the bar drew Wade's gaze. A man he hadn't seen come in was finishing the last swallow of beer in a mug and was rising to leave. Wade turned back to his brother. "That's it, then. Sims, you'll have to show us the way. But first, let's get you cleaned up."

Bronc Long glanced back at the open door of the Casa de León. He was glad that Sims hadn't seen him—which wasn't surprising, considering how far-gone that broken-down drunk was these days.

Bronc smiled as he mounted his black mare. What he had overheard tonight was going to be useful to Frank

McGarth. He spurred the animal south, giving the horse her head. Yes, indeed, Bronc had been at the right place at the right time—and he'd been looking out for Frank's interests. And Frank was generous with men who did that for him.

marked, "but sure I get paid to keep them from talking
enough for anyone else to hear."

One of these worries his brother's blood money
to keep "sure I got no reason to..." they get worried.

Chapter Fifteen

Frank McGarth bit the end from a cigar and spat it to
the floor. He lit the opposite end of the stogie and puffed
twice before looking at Bronc Long. "Just what was so
interesting in town?"

"Sims Wright." A sly smile curled Bronc's lips as
though he concealed a secret.

McGarth hid his disgust behind the cloud of smoke
he exhaled. He did not trust Bronc any more than he
trusted the other men working for him. They were border
trash, all of them. The sooner he could wash his hands of
the whole lot, the safer he'd feel.

In fact, McGarth knew, the sooner he returned to
Waco, the better off he would be. He'd have been there
by now if he had managed to get the army gold. Now he
was stuck here in this godforsaken flea hole, just waiting
for another shipment to be transported to Fort Stockton.

Blowing a stream of blue smoke into the air, McGarth
looked back at his hired gun. "Bronc, tell me why should I
be interested in Sims Wright. I've no use for that drunk."

Bronc's sly smile widened. "Even if he's talkin' to
people?"

McGarth flicked away an ash that fell from the cigar
and settled on the lapel of the white coat he wore. Even if
he was forced to employ a lowlife like Bronc Long, he did
not have to like it. He still thought of himself as a southern gentleman, whatever his surroundings. He played by
a set of rules—his own rules. That made him different
from the Bronc Longs of this world.

"Sims is always talking to people," McGarth com-

mented, "panhandling pennies so he can scrape together
enough for a shot of mescal."

"One of these people is his brother," Bronc replied.

What kind of game was the man playing? McGarth
was surrounded by mental incompetents who tried to
impress him with their intelligence, only to display their
abysmal ignorance and stupidity. "We killed Hap a long
time ago."

"What about *Tom* Wright?" Bronc grinned, revealing
a dark gap where one of his front teeth had been dislodged
in a barroom brawl.

McGarth sat up straight. "Tom Wright? Where did
you hear that name?"

"From one of the men talking with Sims," Bronc
replied. "He drove the stage in from Fort Stockton. The
other man with him was his shotgunner. Roy is what the
others called him, I think."

"Tom Wright? Are you sure?" McGarth demanded.
He knew that name; it took him a second or two to recall
the name of Wright's friend, Roy Calvert.

"I was sittin' as close to them as I am to you now. I
heard all of them call each other by name," Bronc assured
him.

"Tom Wright," McGarth repeated the name. It rolled
over his tongue with a sigh. Wright was a phantom, arisen
from the grave of the past.

Why had Wright returned to Texas? How had he
known to come to Fort Davis? McGarth had no answers
for those questions, but he knew the answer to a third
question: *Why was Wright here?* The answer was obvious:
to find McGarth.

"Where were they when you left town?" he pressed,
doing his best to keep the full measure of his interest from
the man seated across the room.

"Sittin' in the cantina, talkin' about how they was
goin' to ride in here tonight after you," Bronc replied, still
smiling.

McGarth extinguished his cigar in a heavy ashtray on
his desk and then rose to his feet. "I don't think it would
be neighborly to make them wait that long," he said.

"Especially after Tom Wright's come such a long way to pay me a visit. Bronc, tell the other boys to saddle up. We're going into Fort Davis and have ourselves a drink."

Bronc pushed from his chair. His eyes flashed with decided relish. "Rifles and six-shooters?"

"Any weapons they wish to carry," McGarth replied. "This afternoon I intend to do something that I should have done years ago—wipe every last Wright off the face of this earth."

When Bronc started toward the door of the ranch house, McGarth called to him. "Here's a little something in the way of a thank-you."

He flipped a twenty-dollar gold piece to the man. "Tell the others that there's ten of those waiting for the man who brings Tom Wright to me—dead!"

Bronc slipped the gold coin into a shirt pocket and grinned. "My pleasure."

When Bronc left, McGarth edged back his coat and pulled a six-shot revolving Wesson from the holster strapped to his waist. After double-checking the loads, he slapped it back in the holster. The last time he had met Tom Wright— near Sheffield Station, though he hadn't known it at the time—fourteen of his men had died. But then Wright had had other men with him that night, some of them soldiers, and they had taken the camp by surprise. Now, today, McGarth would have all the surprises.

"Damn!" Sims shivered as he glanced up at his brother. "Tom, this water is cold!"

Tom. Wade liked the sound of his own name. However, he could not risk thinking of himself as Tom Wright again. Before the sun rose on another day, he might well have to find himself yet another name—if he lived through what he was planning for tonight.

They were in the barbershop, whose proprietor had thoughtfully rounded up a tub in which Sims was now bathing.

"Pour some more of that hot water in here." Sims pointed to the bucket at his brother's feet. "I can't believe the bathwater is so cold."

It was not, but Wade made no mention of the fact. Instead he lifted the steaming bucket and dumped the water into the tub. In spite of the additional hot water, his brother continued to shiver while he scrubbed himself with a bar of soap. The shaking did not stem from the temperature, Wade realized. Although Sims did his best to conceal it, the man was hurting for a drink.

"Climb on out, dry yourself, and get into those clothes." Wade nodded to the new shirt, pants, and socks Roy held. The clothing had cost Wade two dollars. "You'll be warmer soon as you're dressed."

Sims's shivering doubled when he stepped from the tub. He rubbed himself briskly with the towel Wade handed him, but he was trembling as he put on the clothing. "You were right. I *do* feel better."

Wade smiled to hide the fact that he knew his brother was lying. "Come on, the barber's waiting to give you a shave and a haircut. You'll feel like a new man when he's through with you."

Taking a seat beside Roy on a bench next to the wall, Wade sat while the barber waved Sims to the shop's sole chair. Twenty minutes later Sims, his beard shaven and hair trimmed, resembled a shadow of the young boy Wade remembered.

"I do feel like a new man!" Sims grinned when he pushed from the chair. "Smell as sweet as a rose, too."

His brother was still lying, Wade realized. He seemed to be shaking twice as badly as he had when he stepped from the bath, every muscle in his body quivering as though he were palsied. Wade knew he had to face reality: He could not salvage his brother in one day, not after the man had been lost in a bottle for months on end. It would take days, maybe even weeks, to get him past the shakes, and probably twice that time for him to lose the craving for alcohol. Sims would be of no use to him today or tonight.

"I was thinking that the three of us could use a drink," Wade said, ignoring Roy's raised eyebrows. "Why don't we head back to the cantina?"

"For coffee?" Sims's head turned to his brother.

"Maybe a beer," Wade answered. He saw no need to prolong his brother's suffering.

"No, Tom." Sims shook his head with determination. "I know what you're thinking, and I don't blame you none. I'd probably be thinking the same thing if I was standing in your boots. But you're wrong."

He paused, his fist tightening around the shotgun Roy had given him. "I haven't been this sober in longer than I can remember. Tom, I don't want to go back to where I've been. It's a place that isn't fit for a man. I think that I can make it, if you'll stand by me."

Wade stared at his brother, unable to ignore the quake of his hands. He nodded. "If that's what you want."

"That's what I want." Sims smiled in relief.

"We still have time for that drink," Wade continued. "Only we'll make it coffee all around."

Opening the door of the barbershop, Wade stepped outside. In that single stride, he moved from the adobe structure's cool interior to harsh sunlight. The transition was like climbing from a refreshing mountain stream into a searing oven. He tugged the brim of his hat low to his face to escape the relentless glare of the sun overhead.

The unmistakable crack of a rifle rent the air. A slug of hot lead whined past Wade's right ear to end its flight in a solid thud as it bit into the mud brick, mere inches from the side of his head.

"Back!" Wade did not waste time searching for the cloud of smoke that would betray the rifleman's position. He swirled about and shoved Sims and Roy back into the barbershop as he lunged inside after them.

Two more rifles barked. Bullets ripped into the ground where he had stood but a split second ago, sending clouds of sand and dust into the air.

"I don't want no trouble in my shop!" the barber cried plaintively from behind his chair, where he had crouched for protection. The man's eyes were wide with fear. "You get out of here, you understand? Get out!"

Wade ignored the man. With his back pressed against the front wall of the shop, he inched over to the only window. Roy, in a crouch, crossed to the opposite side of the window. A low whistle escaped his lips. "Somebody is either mighty irritated about the way this barber cuts hair, or I'd say McGarth got wind of the fact that we're in town. I can see about six men from here. All of 'em are spreading out along the street, coming this way, and all of 'em with rifles trained on us."

"It's McGarth," Wade snarled, peering through the window. There was no way he could miss the man. He was standing in front of the cantina, dressed in a white suit and a hat to match, with a smoking rifle in his hands. "He looks mighty cocky, Roy. I'll bet you anything he's got another half dozen men tucked in among the buildings down at that end of town."

"Frank McGarth?" The barber exclaimed. "I don't want no fight with Frank McGarth!" In the next instant the man broke from behind the chair and shot out through the barbershop's back door.

The volley of shots Wade expected to hear as the man was cut down did not come. He glanced at Roy. "Looks like Frank didn't have time to get his men around back, to surround us."

"Or maybe he and his men just ain't got nobody else to cut their hair," Roy replied.

"Wright! Tom Wright!" McGarth called out. "I know you're in there, so listen and listen good. You can have this two ways, easy or hard—"

"Frank's realized his mistake," Roy whispered. "A couple of men down yonder just shot across the street. Won't take 'em long to work up behind us."

"—Come on out and I'll make it quick and easy, the way I did for your pa," McGarth shouted. "But if you make me come in there after you, I guarantee you'll be a long time dying. You hear me, Tom Wright?"

Roy looked at his friend and shrugged, as though asking what he intended.

"Sims, you—" Wade's eyes narrowed. His brother was nowhere to be seen. He drew a deep breath and slowly released it. He could not blame Sims for running; his brother could barely hold on to that shotgun with his shaking hands. He had never expected him actually to fire it.

"Hard or easy, Wright? Which is it going to be?" McGarth demanded. "You got thirty seconds."

"Well?" Roy asked.

"Out the back door," Wade replied as he pushed from the wall. "We don't stand a chance if they pin us down in here."

"That's what I was afraid of," Roy said with a shake of his head. "You always did do things the hard way."

He followed Wade out the back door, where they crouched low, hugging the rear wall of the barbershop.

"Wright," McGarth called. "Time is up! You've made your choice!"

A dozen rifles barked. Glass shattered and bullets whined as they ricocheted off the inner walls of the barbershop. Wade tried not to think about what would have happened had he and Roy remained inside.

Wade's gaze darted left and right. He was looking for the two men that Roy had seen. The question of whether to run from them never entered Wade's mind. Roy and he had to make a stand somewhere, and the two men trying to come up behind them was as good a place to begin as any.

Wade eased the Colt from his belt and cocked the hammer.

"Wright?" McGarth hailed from the street. "Wright?"

Wade caught sight of a storage bin located behind a blacksmith shop two buildings away. Men coming from that direction, trying to reach the barbershop, would have to pass between that bin and the blacksmith shop. He nudged Roy and pointed. "Behind there."

Roy required no further explanation. He ran at Wade's side, and they dropped behind the bin. The two men who had moved in from the street were nowhere in sight. When Roy looked at his friend questioningly, all he received in answer was an uncertain shake of Wade's head.

"All right, boys," McGarth ordered his men, "put another round through the window!"

Man-made thunder rolled through the town's streets

as McGarth and his men unleashed their rifles for a second time. Again the whine of ricocheting lead sounded from within the barbershop as the hail of bullets peppered the building's interior.

Neither Wade nor Roy had time to glance back at the shop. The volley apparently also served as a signal to the two men Roy had spotted earlier. The instant the first rifle shot cracked, the men came around the back of a dressmaker's store three buildings away from the storage bin. Both men held six-shooters ready as they ran toward the rear of the barbershop.

"I'll take the first one," Roy whispered.

Wade offered no protest. Raising his Colt, he sighted on the second man, waiting until his target ran past the bin. He squeezed down on the trigger the moment Roy's Remington barked.

The .44-caliber slug caught Wade's man in midstride. The impact of the shot hurled him against the wall of the blacksmith's shop. He slid down the unpainted boards, leaving a smear of red on the wood, and died two feet from Roy's man, who lay face down in the sand.

"Two down," Roy said grimly. "Damn. I wish they had been carrying rifles. We could use them right now."

Wade tapped his friend's shoulder as he pushed from behind the bin and moved to the dead men. Although the two did not have rifles, they did carry pistols. He picked up both, stuffing one into his belt and tossing the other to Roy. Wade then pointed to the dressmaker's shop the men had come from. Without a word they dashed around the building and edged toward the street.

When they reached it, Wade peered cautiously to the left and right. They were now several buildings closer to the cantina.

"McGarth's men have gone by us," Wade turned and whispered to Roy. "They're closing in on the barbershop."

"And they ain't gonna be none too happy when they find we ain't inside," Roy replied. "Or when they discover the little surprise we left out back."

Wade agreed as he watched McGarth and his band of hired guns creep closer to the barbershop. He had to take advantage of the shock McGarth would receive when he looked into the shop.

Scanning the stores across the street, Wade saw an open space between a feed store and a farm-implement store, directly across from the barbershop. The narrow space would offer a clear line of fire on McGarth's men. The problem was getting there.

Quickly he made up his mind. "I'm going to try for the other side," he told Roy. He barely thought about the foolishness of what he was planning: Even though he'd be running behind McGarth and his men, any one of them could hear him, turn, and cut him down with a hail of lead.

"You're not going without me!" Roy hissed.

Both men broke into a dead run and shot for the store immediately across the street, a land office. Their breath came quick and shallow as they ducked around the side of the building.

Wade did not pause to consider how they had made it across without being heard. That they had done so was enough for now. Moving behind the land office, he quickly ran toward the rear of the feed store, Roy at his heels.

When they reached the narrow space that they had seen from across the street, Wade stopped and glanced at his companion, who nodded that he understood what his friend had in mind.

"Wright!" Anger brimmed in McGarth's voice. "It won't do you any good to run. There's no place you can hide from me in this town!"

"Reckon he looked inside the barbershop and noticed we weren't there." Roy shrugged.

"Might as well let him know where we are."

Together Wade and Roy stepped into the space between the buildings. They had a direct bead on McGarth and his men, who stood in a tight group in front of the barbershop.

Wade and Roy raised their pistols. In rapid succession their revolvers fired three rounds each. Before the smoke cleared, the two men had swung back behind the cover of the feed store.

A yowl of pain, just before a volley of rifle shots answered their unexpected attack, announced that at least one of their bullets had found a target.

"Spread out and get them!" McGarth screamed his order. "I'll give three hundred dollars to the man who gets Wright!"

Roy's eyebrows arched. "That's almost enough to make a man reconsider which side of this fight he should be on."

Wade paid his friend no heed. The crunch of sand beneath boots came from both sides. McGarth's men had crossed the street and started to work around the buildings. Roy and he would be caught in a crossfire if they remained here. But there was nowhere to run; the open land that stretched to the east offered no shelter.

"The roof," Roy said, pointing overhead.

"Can we get up there?"

"Just watch me." Roy jumped up with the grace of a cat, easily catching hold of the edge of the roof and chinning himself upward. Then he eased first one leg and the other onto the rooftop. He turned around and reached down.

Wade waved the arm away. There was no time. The sound of approaching boots was too close. He had no desire for a slug to catch him while he dangled halfway to the roof. Instead he dropped to his stomach and rolled beneath the feed store, pulling himself into the crawl space that separated the floor of the wooden building from the sandy ground.

His position gave him an unrestricted, ground-level view across the street. His and Roy's shots had found more than one target: Three men lay sprawled in front of the barbershop. He also saw the boots of two men who were creeping along each side of the feed store. He watched them reach the rear corners of the building, halt, then quickly step around.

He hoped against hope that the men would fire on each other, but they did not. Instead, they pivoted and hastily strode back toward the street.

The man to Wade's left called out, "They ain't here, Frank. Ain't hide nor hair of them!"

"They couldn't have vanished into thin air, Chris! Get back there and find them, you jackass!" McGarth shouted at the man.

A half-muffled groan and the scuffle of boots jerked Wade's head to the right. The gunman toppled to the ground, a knife jutting from his back. Behind the dead man, he saw Roy's scarred boots, watched as his friend wrenched his blade from between the man's ribs and then leapt upward to regain the roof.

Roy had done his part to lessen the odds; now it was Wade's turn. He looked back to the left. The man McGarth had called Chris once more walked toward the back of the feed store, turned the corner, and edged along the rear wall.

Wade inched toward the open side of the crawl space, waited for the man to pass, and then rolled out.

"Chris!" he called to the man's back.

The gunman spun around. Wade fired. The shot struck dead center of the man's chest. Wade did not wait to watch the man fall. Continuing to roll, he disappeared into the crawl space beneath the farm-implement store.

Four shots rang out to his right. A man cried out in pain. Before his mind could form Roy's name, he heard the sound of boots running across the feed store's roof. The footsteps abruptly stopped and were followed by a heavy thud far above his head.

Wade smiled. Not only did Roy live, but he had now moved from one rooftop to the other to continue his aerial assault. High and low, he thought. It was time for him to strike from ground level again.

He glanced to his left. No one was moving along the opposite side of the implement store.

But when he looked to the street once more, he cursed silently. Directly across the street he saw white pant legs. *McGarth!*

Reversing his direction, Wade rolled from under the store and crouched beside its wall. Glancing at the street, he saw that he was out of McGarth's line of sight.

Checking his Colt, he found one shot remaining in the cylinder. He broke open the weapon and replaced the

all but spent cylinder with the fully loaded one he carried
in his pocket. He then checked the unfired Remington
under his belt; five rounds remained in the pistol. He
slipped the Remington back under his belt and crept
between the buildings toward the street.

"Damn!" The curse hissed from his lips.

The street lay empty. McGarth was nowhere in sight.
Nor were any of the five men who remained with him.
Where had they gone? Wade looked left and then right—
nothing, not even a sound.

Cocked Colt held ready, he stepped from between
the buildings onto the street. Where was Roy? He scanned
the rooftops and saw nothing. Hunter and hunted, he
slowly moved toward the center of the small town. His
gaze ran along the storefronts on both sides of the street—
still nothing. Where were they?

The front door of a general store across the street
creaked open. Frank McGarth abruptly stepped onto the
street. Wade swung to face the man, and then a blur of
motion closer to him caught the corner of his left eye.
Trap!

There was no time to think. Wade threw himself flat
to the ground. The report of two pistols roared. The air
sizzled as two slugs whined harmlessly above him. McGarth
had been no more than a decoy, for while he had drawn
Wade's attention across the street, two gunmen on this
side had slipped out of a newspaper office, intent on
taking Wade from behind.

Twisting about, Wade whipped the Colt around. He
pointed the revolver at the two dark forms half hidden in a
cloud of gunsmoke. Twice he squeezed the trigger. Both
men groaned and staggered backward under the hammering impact of hot lead. They fell, their bodies twitching as
life fled them.

Wade rolled back to his stomach to level the Colt at
McGarth. The doorway was empty; the man had disappeared again!

Rising from the sand, Wade sprinted across the street.
Like a charging bull, he ran through the open door.
McGarth was not inside. A back door that swayed in the

afternoon breeze gave evidence of a hasty exit. Wade crossed to the door and peered outside.

A hundred yards to his left he saw and heard the back door of the church close. A humorless smile lifted his lips. McGarth moved too slowly. Not even a church could hide him now.

With a glance from side to side to make certain McGarth's gunmen did not wait beyond the door to greet him, Wade darted from the store and ran toward the steepled church. Four gunshots echoed in the distance. He shoved to the back of his mind the possibility that one of those shots had taken Roy. If one had, it was too late for him to do anything about it now. His task was to find McGarth and make certain that neither his friend nor he had died in vain this day.

Wade's outstretched fingers were a mere inch from the church door's latch when he caught himself. Surely McGarth expected him to follow, and just as surely the man waited for the back door to open so that he could pick Wade off as he stepped over the threshold.

Backing away from the obvious trap, Wade turned, rounded the corner, and moved along the side of the church. Double-checking the street, he climbed to the wide porch in front and crept to a pair of doors, the main entrance to the church. As quietly as possible, he turned the two brass handles. Then he stepped out of the line of fire and used a boot toe to nudge both doors open.

Nothing!

The thunder of exploding black powder he had expected did not come. Not even a creak of settling boards came from within.

Two more shots echoed down the street.

Wade jumped in spite of himself. A quick glance down the sandy avenue revealed neither Roy nor any of McGarth's men. Wade looked back to the two doors that now stood wide open. His surprise attack had failed. There was only one way to find out if McGarth remained inside. Wade sucked down a steadying breath and ran through the open doors.

At the opposite end of the church, near the altar,

blue and yellow flame blazed as a gun was fired, its report reverberating off the walls. A foot to Wade's right the back of a pew exploded, showering splinters into the air, as lead bit into the wood.

Wade's Colt's leapt up Three times the muzzle spoke as Wade sprayed lead at the blaze that had blossomed out of the church's dim light. A man cried out, and Wade immediately squeezed off the last round in the cylinder. He heard a groan and then the heavy sound of a man dropping to the wooden floor.

Wrenching the Remington from his belt, he moved forward. A man lay sprawled facedown, unmoving, in front of the altar. It was not McGarth. The patterned shirt and dark pants the man wore were all Wade needed to see to know that.

"Drop the pistol, Wright." McGarth's voice came from behind Wade. "Do it now. I want to watch you die slowly, but if you move, I'll put a bullet between your shoulder blades right now."

The Remington slipped from Wade's fingers, thudding to the floor. His blood running cold, he turned slowly. Frank McGarth stepped out of the pews he had hidden among when Wade had entered the church. He held a Wesson, its muzzle aimed directly at Wade's chest. A wide grin spread across the man's face as his finger tightened around the trigger.

A flower of yellow and blue blossomed from the barrel of McGarth's pistol. Pain lanced through Wade's right arm as lead tore into flesh and muscle like a white-hot brand. The impact spun him around and back against the raised pulpit. Clutching the arm with his left hand, he managed to right himself and turn to face McGarth again.

"It hurts, doesn't it, Tom? I can see the hurt on your face. I like that. I want you to hurt."

Wade gritted his teeth, trying to fight past the throbbing pain that seared through his arm and shoulder. McGarth's eyes gleamed as he stared at him. Frank's expression was one that Wade had seen before, one usually reserved for the pleasure a man took in a woman, not from inflicting agony in others.

"I should have killed you that night back in Waco, Tom, the same way I killed your father and your brother Hap. But I was as young as you then. I thought it would be cleaner if I made it look like you had killed Ben Alexander. I didn't take into account the possibility of your escaping the law. I won't make that mistake this time—"

McGarth's grin widened when Wade tried to move his arm. He could not. He attempted to flex the muscles, and something felt as though it was tearing within the arm. In spite of himself, he groaned.

"—That's just the beginning, Tom. Today, I'm going to do what I should have done five years ago. I'm going to kill you. And like I promised, your dying is going to come hard. First I'm going to put a slug in your other arm. Then with the next two shots, I'll take off your knee caps. The fifth shot goes into your gut. You'll be begging me for the last bullet, which I'll place right between your eyes."

Wade's eyes darted around the church looking for an avenue of escape. There was none. Even the Remington that lay two feet from his boots was too far away to reach before McGarth could pull the trigger again.

The shuffle of boots on wood came from the front of the church. Wade's gaze shot to the opened doors. The twisted form of a man stood silhouetted by the sun outside. *Sims!*

Sims held Roy's shotgun in his good hand. Both of the hammers were cocked. "Toss down the gun, Frank."

Dammit, thought Wade. *Why did he open his mouth?*

In one fluid motion, McGarth swirled and fired.

A split second later both barrels of the scattergun roared, the buckshot peppering not McGarth but the church's ceiling as Sims tumbled back, a death cry tearing from his lips.

"No!" Wade screamed. He had searched for a way to escape McGarth, but he had never reckoned on paying such a heavy price for that chance. Now he had to make certain that Sims had not died in vain.

Dropping to his knees, Wade scooped up the Remington with his left hand. Awkwardly he thumbed back the hammer and swung the pistol toward McGarth. The man spun around in time to take Wade's first shot in the chest. The second round Wade fired hit him in the forehead. McGarth fell like a toppled oak, his unseeing eyes staring at the ceiling.

Wade forced himself to stand. McGarth was dead, but the others were still outside. He had to get to them before they found Roy—if Roy was still alive. He took one step toward the front door and froze.

A man stepped over the threshold and leveled a pistol at him.

Chapter Sixteen

"**L**et it fall, Wright. You've no reason for the gun now. He was the last of them."

Thacker! Wade's grip tightened around the Remington's butt.

"I said drop it." Matthew Thacker's tone left no doubt that if necessary he would use the pistol he held. "You and your friend got them all. McGarth there was the last. Like I said, you've got no need for the gun. Unless you're planning to have a go at me?"

Wade opened his left hand, letting the Remington drop to the floor. He had completed all he had come to Fort Davis to do—his gaze dropped to Sims's lifeless body—and at a price higher than he had ever thought possible. The fight had gone out of him. There would be no more killing today, not by his hand.

"What now?" Wade looked back at Thacker, who was carefully easing down the hammer of his pistol.

Before Thacker could answer, a cry was heard from the street. "Wade!" It was Laura's voice. "Wade, are you all right?"

The young woman burst through the open door and pushed past the former Ranger without a glance at the gun in his hand.

Roy followed her. For him, Thacker's drawn weapon was more than obvious. He skidded to a halt, his gaze shifting between Wade and Thacker. Roy's right hand drifted toward the Remington tucked beneath his belt. Wade shook his head, warning his friend off.

"Oh, Wade!" Laura threw her arms around Wade's

180

neck. Her lips pressed all over his face at once while tears streamed down her cheeks. "I heard the shooting, and I ran all the way from the fort. I was so afraid you had gotten yourself killed. When I thought you might be dead— well, I just saw everything clearly—oh, Wade, God, how I love you!"

She smothered his face in another barrage of kisses. "I meant it when I said the past doesn't matter to me. All that matters is that we're together. I want to be with you, Wade, no matter what happens."

Wade's left arm tightened around her waist, and he smiled down at her, relief and joy in his face. Then his gaze darkened and lifted to Thacker. "Well, I reckon what happens next will be up to Mr. Thacker here—and to a judge."

Laura stared at Wade as though confused by his meaning. She followed his gaze to Thacker, noticing for the first time the gun the man still held. "What's going on?"

Thacker glanced down at his pistol. He quickly slipped the weapon back into its holster. "What, Tom—Wade—"

"Tom," Tom Wright corrected. There was no need to hide behind the name Wade Bonner anymore.

"—Tom," Thacker continued, "is trying to say is that he has a few legal matters he has to clear up back in Austin."

Laura's face paled as Thacker's meaning sank in. "You've come after him, haven't you?"

"That's the way it is," Thacker answered. "There's an outstanding murder warrant with Tom Wright's name on it."

"But he didn't kill that man. Frank McGarth did," Laura protested, clinging tighter to Tom.

"I know," Thacker said.

Tom's head jerked up. "You know?"

Thacker looked at McGarth's body. "McGarth there was a man of many words. I heard every one he said to you—how he killed Ben Alexander in Waco as well as your father and brother Hap. I saw him gun down Sims. I think a judge would rule that a dying man's confession is admissible and definitive, especially if I were the one who told him that that was the way it happened."

Tom studied the man. "Just what are you getting at?"

"I heard everything that McGarth said before he died, right here in this church," Thacker replied. "He confessed to framing you for the murder of Ben Alexander. You're innocent, and I know that. Now, a court still must clear the charges against you, but if you'll return with me to Austin, I'll testify in your behalf. I don't think there'll be any difficulty in straightening out a few kinks in justice's tail."

Laura's emerald eyes rolled up to Tom, filled with hope.

Wade returned her gaze. He had denied her once; he could not do it again. He looked at Thacker and nodded. "I'll come with you. There won't be any need for manacles or leg irons."

Thacker smiled. "I didn't think there would." He paused, looking Wade in the eyes. "You know, after you saved my son, I knew that whatever business remained between us was going to end, and for the best. Thanks, friend." He extended his hand to Wade, who grasped it firmly.

Thacker turned to Laura. "Ma'am, I promise I won't keep him away a moment longer than is necessary. He should be back inside of a month."

"And when I come back, I'll be able to offer you my real name on a marriage license, not 'Wade Bonner.' " He leaned down and sealed that promise with a kiss.

Thacker motioned Wright to the door. "We'll stop by the fort and let the surgeon take a look at that arm before we head back to Austin."

Tom stopped as he walked outside, bent down, and closed Sim's eye with his left hand. He looked at Thacker. "You think we could take the time to give him a decent burial? He deserves that."

"I agree," Thacker said. "We'll do it."

Two hours later, in the graveyard behind the church, Tom, Roy, Laura, and Thacker gently eased Sims's body into the ground. A pine box had been found, a grumbling church sexton had helped dig the grave, and now it was done. Tom tossed the first clump of earth on the rough pine boards, then others followed suit. When they turned away, the sexton and his assistant, a boy of twelve, began to finish filling in the grave.

"The stage," Tom said, as they walked out of the churchyard. "You can handle the team, Roy."

"I'd like to take you along as shotgunner." Roy shrugged.

"Ask Mr. Dalrymple. He seems to be able to handle a gun."

Tom walked down the street at Thacker's side to their horses. He looked back at the church as he mounted a chestnut filly. Laura and Roy stood in the street watching. He turned away. In that direction lay the future. It did not belong to him yet, but it would. First he had the past to lay to rest.

"Ready?" Thacker climbed astride his bay.

Tom nodded. "The sooner we get started, the sooner I'll be back."

He glanced over his shoulder at the future one more time before reining the chestnut toward the fort. A smile danced at the corners of his mouth. For the first time in more years than he liked to remember, he had a future. That thought alone was enough to keep him going for the next month.

THE EXCITING NEW FRONTIER SERIES
BY THE CREATORS OF
WAGONS WEST
STAGECOACH
by Hank Mitchum

"The STAGECOACH series is great frontier entertainment. Hank Mitchum really makes the West come alive in each story."
> —Dana Fuller Ross, author of *Wagons West*

★ WAGONS WEST ★

A series of unforgettable books that trace the lives of a dauntless band of pioneering men, women, and children as they brave the hazards of an untamed land in their trek across America. This legendary caravan of people forge a new link in the wilderness. They are Americans from the North and the South, alongside immigrants, Blacks, and Indians, who wage fierce daily battles for survival on this uncompromising journey—each to their private destinies as they fulfill their greatest dreams.

☐	26822	INDEPENDENCE! #1	$4.50
☐	26162	NEBRASKA! #2	$4.50
☐	26242	WYOMING! #3	$4.50
☐	26072	OREGON! #4	$4.50
☐	26070	TEXAS! #5	$4.50
☐	26377	CALIFORNIA! #6	$4.50
☐	26546	COLORADO! #7	$4.50
☐	26069	NEVADA! #8	$4.50
☐	26163	WASHINGTON! #9	$4.50
☐	26073	MONTANA! #10	$4.50
☐	26184	DAKOTA! #11	$4.50
☐	26521	UTAH! #12	$4.50
☐	26071	IDAHO! #13	$4.50
☐	26367	MISSOURI! #14	$4.50
☐	27141	MISSISSIPPI! #15	$4.50
☐	25247	LOUISIANA! #16	$4.50
☐	25622	TENNESSEE! #17	$4.50
☐	26022	ILLINOIS! #18	$4.50
☐	26533	WISCONSIN! #19	$4.50
☐	26849	KENTUCKY! #20	$4.50
☐	27065	ARIZONA! #21	$4.50
☐	27458	NEW MEXICO! #22	$4.50

Prices and availability subject to change without notice.

- -

Bantam Books, Dept. LE, 414 East Golf Road, Des Plaines, IL 60016

Please send me the books I have checked above. I am enclosing $_____ (please add $2.00 to cover postage and handling). Send check or money order—no cash or C.O.D.s please.

Mr/Ms _____

Address _____

City/State _____ Zip _____

LE—4/89

Please allow four to six weeks for delivery. This offer expires 10/89.